The Tale of Tyrfing

By Sokarjo Stormwillow

The Tale of Tyrfing

PENDRAIG
PENDRAIG Publishing
Los Angeles, California

The Tale of Tyrfing
By Sokarjo Stormwillow
First Edition © 2010
by PENDRAIG Publishing
All rights reserved.

No part of this publication may be reproduced, stored in a retrieval system or transmitted in any form or by any means, electronic, mechanical, photocopying, recording or otherwise without the prior written permission of the copyright holder, except brief quotation in a review.

Cover Design &
Interior Typeset & Layout   Jo-Ann Byers Mierzwicki

PENDRAIG Publishing
Sunland, CA 91040
http://www.PendraigPublishing.com
Printed in the United States of America

ISBN: 978-0-9843302-4-9

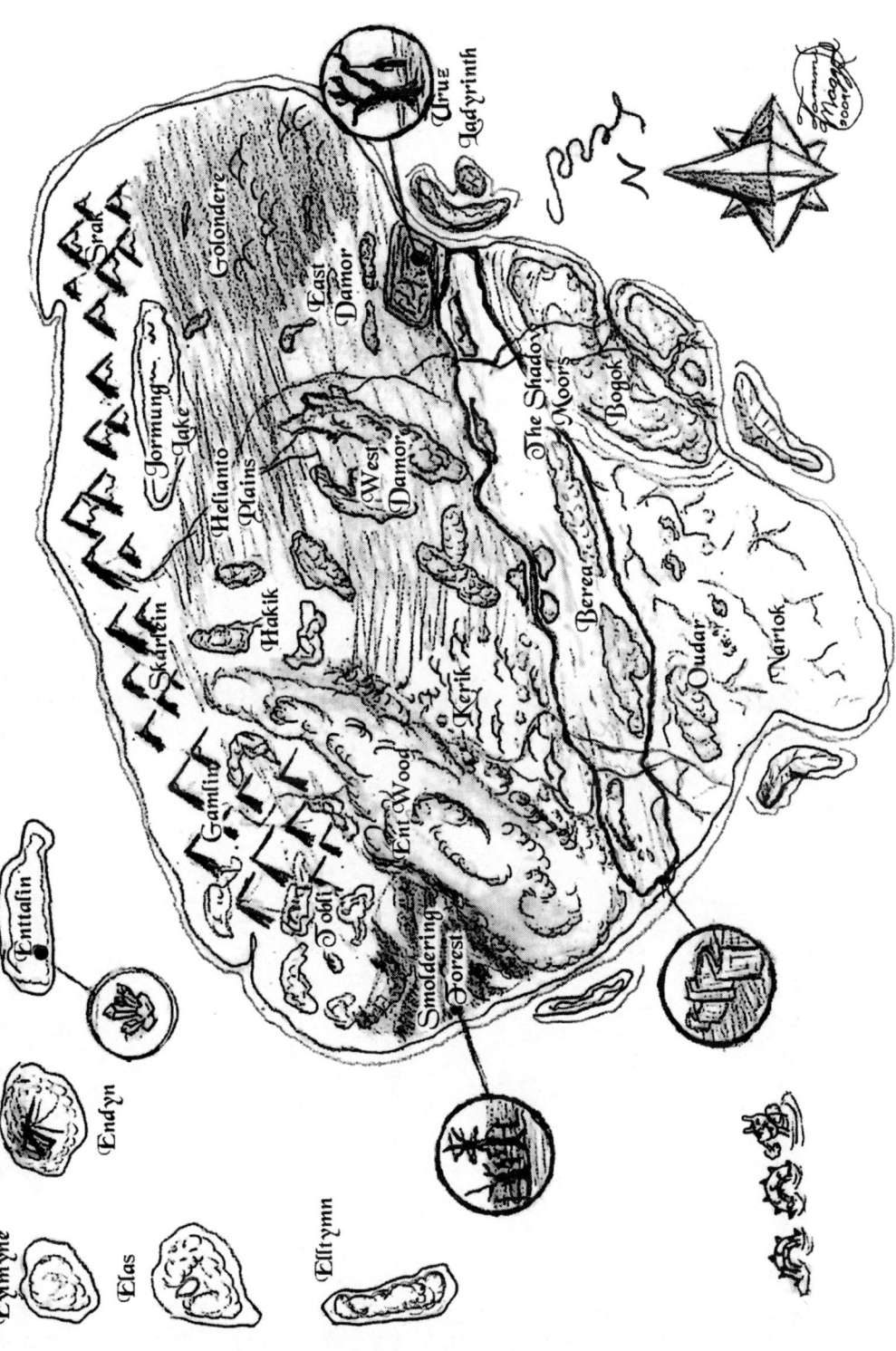

Chapter One

Year 67 of the Shadow Age,
The Lost Continent of Piyr
Midgard

The snow was falling in gentle flakes, coating the crude burlap tents with a soft, light powder and melting onto the noses of the sweaty men as they built their meager shelters. Dozens of dead carcasses, mostly of foxes and wolves, lay piled on the stained snow close to the tents, waiting to be robbed of their skins. The sun was drifting slowly toward the horizon, and soft pinks and golds illuminated the sky, deepening their hues as the moments vanished. The clouds moved closer toward the mountains of Gamlin, leaving a blanket of sparkling snowflakes, catching the fading sun's last rays and glimmering like diamonds. The disheveled tents stood scattered in the rugged form of a half circle in a large clearing surrounded by tall pine and cedar trees. The men, giant in stature and rough in manner, began gathering around the large fire in the center of the camp. One fur-clad man was hungrily jabbing a dirty halberd at a large slab of meat slung over logs above the blaze. Most of the men carried halberds or spears, the metal of which was filthy and the wood splintered. Others wore old swords swinging loosely at their sides. All were clad in the brown and black furs of different animals, bound to their massive bodies with leather straps and belts. They began rubbing their hands together and licking their lips, crowding around the meat like vultures. The smell of the meat roasting above the fire drifted along the crisp cold air and filtered into the forest, sifting through the natural smells of evergreen needles and bark. Woodpeckers echoed in the trees and an occasional cry from a hawk echoed through the mountain air. One man looked up as a giant figure strode slowly away from the camp.

"Grimfar! Where you goin'? We're just gettin' ready to eat!" The figure stopped and turned.

"Meat of bear good for barbarian. Grimfar need sometin' good for troll." The emerald giant turned and sauntered away from the camp.

"Well, suit yourself. Your loss." The other barbarians chuckled and turned back to their steaming dinner.

The troll strolled into the nearby wood, walking slowly, his large black eyes searching the ground. His sword hung loosely upon his back and he carried a spear in one hand. His hair, coarse and matted, was too rough to be blown in the gentle mountain breeze that whispered through the pines, though it was long and rested on his broad, muscled shoulders. His greenish skin was caked with grime and dirt, and his gator-skin armored clothing was torn and smelled fouler than any of the barbarians could have despaired to smell. But he cared not. Why should he? He was a troll, after all, and trolls care nothing for grace or scent or even for cleanliness. The only thing that was playing about in this troll's mind was the thought of his next meal.

Then he froze, each muscle in his body stiff as if turned to stone. Jerking suddenly, he stabbed his spear into the half-frozen earth. Lifting his spear, he pulled a wriggling, two-foot worm out of the rich soil. The giant grub seemed to shrink in his enormous hands as he slid it off the tip of his spear.

"Now dis good food for Grimfar. Mud slug!"

Back at the camp, the barbarians were seated on huge logs and stumps, scraping the last of the bear meat from their greasy iron plates. The wind had picked up after the snow stopped falling and the air was getting colder as the winter sun sank below the regal pines.

"Elrik, where we goin' from here?" a man asked, tossing his empty dish into a pot half-filled with boiling water, which was hung above a small fire. The metal dish landed with a splash and a hiss and others began tossing their plates into the pot as well. The man knelt close to his leader and began scooping snow into his hands to remove the dried bear blood.

"Well, Kalin," the red-bearded man answered, an obvious lover of talk. "From Gamlin, we'll travel south through the Entas Wood. We'll cut 'cross Kerik into Berea where we'll sell our furs and head home to Srak." He leaned back, slapped the man on the back and grinned, clearly pleased with himself.

"Why Kerik, Elrik?" a man nearby asked, as he ran a sharpening stone across the blade of his broadsword.

"To see the king, of course. King Terek is sending King Ricaud of Kerik a gift." Elrik declared, standing to his feet and crossing quickly over the now-packed snow to the questioning hunter. Leaning close to the startled man's face he sneered. "Perhaps you'd rather go through the Smolderin' Forest and be ambushed by bloody drows, eh? Ha-ha!" Elrik straightened up and crossed his arms with a grin. "Even with Grimfar along we'd have quite a time of it in there."

"Where'd Grimfar come from, Elrik?" Kalin asked. "For as long as I can remember, he's always just been there."

The Tale of Tyrfing

"Well," the leader began, pacing back and forth in front of the larger fire, delighted at the prospect of a tale. "Years and years ago, a large army of our men went down to Bogok and wiped out an entire city of trolls. My father was too young to go at the time, but my grandfather went and he said it was glorious! I still remember his tales of the blood... the carnage... the victory!"

A grey-haired hunter leaned close to another and said quietly, "I'll bet he used just as many words, too." The men near him chuckled, but Elrik ignored them and continued his story.

"Well, accordin' to my grandfather, a small band of trolls escaped. These trolls tracked them north, all the way to the Helianto Plains. But the land and air was too hot for 'em an' they went runnin' back to Bogok. One of 'em, though, got lost in the grasslands and died. My grandfather came 'cross it when he was huntin' alone. He said it looked as scary as Brollen on a bad hair day and smelled a whole lot worse!" The camp roared with laughter, quieted by a raised hand from the grinning Elrik. "But he walked right up to it. Come to find out it was a female troll and she had a baby troll with her." Here the red-bearded man paused and added, thoughtfully, "can't quite figure what a woman would be doin' with a group of scoundrels out huntin' men, even a troll one." Shaking his head, he continued with more resolve. "But I 'spose we got us one, too. Anyhow, my grandfather felt sorry for the tyke an' he took the little guy home to my grandmother. Well she was madder'n a nest a goblins when she saw what he brought home! But after a couple a days a makin' him sleep outside, she fin'lly decided to take care of the little tyke."

"She left the baby outside?" Kalin asked, shocked.

"Of course not, idiot! My grandfather!" The men roared again.

After the clamor had subsided, Kalin asked another question. "So if he grew up with your grandfather, how come he's such a good tracker? Your sire couldn't track a beast if it bit 'im in the knee!" Another bout of laughter quickly quieted down by a sour look from Elrik.

"He learned from Elder Hopforn, best tracker in Piyr!"

"Speakin' of babies, why'n the world did ya let Odenia and that baby come with us, Elrik?" an uneasy hunter wondered.

"Because, Hagder," Elrik said, impatiently. "Odenia just so happens to be the best shaman in Srak and she's married to the best hunter in Srak!"

"Besides, Hagder," another man spoke up. "Ya need someone to sing ya to sleep." Laughter echoed through the camp.

Flustered, Hagder retorted, "but she's a woman!"

"Well she's got more guts than you do, Hagder Frig!" the leader bellowed. "Besides, if I hadn't let her come, Brollen wouldn't 'ave come, and we need him on this trip. He'll take care a' her and the baby no need to fret 'bout that."

"So we hope," the doubtful barbarian grumbled, running a rough hand through his feathery, straw-colored locks.

"Oh stop yer belly-achin', Hagder," a handsome man chided. He dusted off his fur cap then slapped it back onto his head with a grin. "Ain't much'll bother us when we got a troll along."

Elrik grinned devilishly. He strode a few steps to the most cheerful fellow of the group and leaned close to the grinning man's tanned face, his amber eyes alight with the fire of a storyteller. "Ya best be glad we ain't going through Bogok, eh?" The laughter quieted down, though there were still grins on every face. "Why, only things we'd hafta worry 'bout is frogmen an' snakes an' gators, right?" Now even the smiles were diminishing. "Oh, an' trolls, of course. Only these trolls aren't like Grimfar, are they? They're heartless beasts! They'll tear your eyes out and feed 'em to the birds! They'll rip your head off and toss it in their soup!" Elrik's breathing got faster as he spoke, his voice louder and louder.

"Elrik! Elrik!" Jyste shouted. "Elrik, calm yourself! Elrik, your losin' it! Just relax a bit, eh?"

Elrik's heavy breathing gradually slackened, and he relaxed his tense muscles, though only slightly. He paused, looked around, and then sighed anxiously. "Aye. Jyste... It's just... there's somethin' in the air. Somethin' doesn't feel right. Don't know what's wrong. Listen." The men paused, unsure of what to listen for. "Hear that? Even the birds've gone quiet. Somethin's goin' on an' I don't like it!"

It was true. The woods were silent now; even the crickets had ceased their songs. The hunters looked uneasily towards the forest.

And deep within the evergreen boughs – something stirred.

A tall, elegant woman with wheat-colored waves cascading onto her fur-clad shoulders, and emerald eyes glistening playfully beneath long dark lashes, hid behind a thick bush laden with bluish-black berries and freshly fallen snow. She giggled softly as she heard footsteps crunching the snow nearby. Stepping blithely out from the shelter of the thicket, she cast dancing eyes toward the figure she had thought was her teasing husband. It was not and her scream pierced the frigid air, though not quite reaching the straining ears of the anxious men in the camp.

A baby's gurgle startled the fretting men, and Jyste sighed, sheathed his sword and strode a few steps toward the baby's tent.

"Hey Jyste! Where's Odenia and Brollen anyhow?" Kalin called after him.

"Who knows? Left an hour ago to find some berries or somethin' for the baby. Haven't seen 'em ba...."

"Brollen!" a man wailed suddenly. Jyste spun around and saw a bloodied body limping towards the camp. An enormous barbarian held

The Tale of Tyrfing

his bleeding side, groaned, then dropped to his knees on the snow just outside the camp. Blood trickled down his bulky arms and his long black ponytail onto the pure whiteness of the soft mounds as the burly man fell to his side with a moan. The men rushed to him, fear leaping to their eyes. Elrik was the first to reach him, but as his hands touched Brollen's body, the wounded man screamed and twisted onto his back. The men leapt back, leaving Elrik kneeling next to the screaming man, staring in shock. Brollen's bloodied skin began melting away as if under extreme heat. Elrik fell back, barely catching himself with his arms and sat, still staring, unbelieving. Brollen's eyes rolled back in his head then vanished. As the melting skin touched the snow, steam hissed up, swirling around his rotting flesh. His arms and legs jerked as he continued screaming and his skin ran off and vanished into the red-stained snow. In seconds, all that was left of the great barbarian was a skeleton, open-mouthed, bereft of all muscle and flesh. The men stared, barely breathing, at the bones of their once gallant friend.

Elrik finally looked up at his frightened men. "This place is cursed," he whispered.

Suddenly, as if Elrik's voice had awoken it, the skeleton swung its arm and grabbed Elrik's throat. With one quick jerk, the creature snapped his neck then dropped his lifeless form onto the snow beside it. The men instantly leapt into action, angry at the loss of both their valued comrade and their trusted leader. Unsheathing their hunting knives and hand axes, they rushed at the skeleton, now standing over its victim's dead body.

Suddenly, they froze, watching in helpless terror as the skeleton began transforming before their eyes. A greenish light swirled about the legs of the skeleton, rising to cover his entire body. A small blast of light revealed, not a blood-stained skeleton, but a slender dark elf, clothed in a deep, rich black robe, grinning mockingly at the barbarians before him.

"This place is not cursed." The voice deep and threatening, smooth and calm. "You are."

"Who are you, drow? What do you want?" questioned Kalin, his hands shaking.

"Your demise," the dark elf answered, his deep purple eyes angrily glaring at the trembling warrior. He pulled both arms from behind his back and raised them high into the air. In one hand he clutched a long, black, bloodied ponytail. A black band, once gracing the ankle of a barbarian maiden, rested on his wrist, a sickening trophy for the murder of a gentle woman.

Instantly Kalin screamed and fell to his knees, dropping his hand ax and clenching his stomach. He too twisted onto his back, screaming in agonizing pain as his skin and muscle vanished. When all that was left was a skeleton, Jyste turned on the dark elf and charged, his short sword lifted above his head, his war cry filling the still air. The dark elf said nothing, his eyes laughing mockingly.

Jyste cried out, clutching his side, and fell to the ground. Instantly the others did the same and the small camp was filled with the screams of the men as their flesh melted away.

In the frozen forest, Grimfar was slurping the last of his messy meal and tossing the head aside when he heard the most terrifying scream ever to land on his ears during his entire long trollish life. He leapt to his feet, pausing and listening carefully. The sound was coming from the camp and the troll dashed forward, racing through the snowy forest toward the scream. Seconds later more screams filled the air, then more, until Grimfar thought his eardrums would burst. His heart pounded as he ran, his blood rushing through his veins until the throb of his head nearly drowned out the sound of the screaming.

At the camp, the drow drew close to Jyste, who was still barely alive, but writhing in anguished pain. He grabbed a fistful of ruddy brown hair and pulled Jyste's head back, forcing the barbarian to look into his mocking face.

"You are brave, son of Srak, but might alone will never stop me. Nothing will ever stop me."

Jyste spat into the dark elf's face then gasped for air. "I have heard of you, foul villain. Our lives... will be... avenged. Your time... will come!" With his last wailing words, Jyste shrieked, his eyes bulging and his chest heaving upwards, struggling for air. The drow straightened up and stepped back, a look of scorn and hatred on his face. He stretched out his palms over the dying man and a pale green light glowed about them. Jyste's screams became louder and more intense as his flesh burst into flames.

"You are wrong, weakling. This is my time."

Suddenly, the mountainside became deathly silent. Grimfar slowed to a stop as he entered the camp, sword drawn. Bones and rotting flesh littered the ground. Grimfar saw the body of Elrik and rushed to his side. When he raised him up with one hand, Elrik's head rolled to one side, threatening to rip completely off. Grimfar quickly dropped him. The troll stood, staring in stunned anger and grief at the dry bones and corpses of his companions.

Enraged, he let out a terrifying roar that seemed to cause the very mountains themselves to shiver.

Already miles away, the dark elf stopped and turned. "A troll?" he murmured to himself. "What could a troll be doing out here?" He paused thoughtfully for a moment then shrugged. "Ah, well. My minions likely find him." He held his hands over the snowy earth and the sickly green light churned round the slender fingers. A large bear appeared, eyes glowing red,

The Tale of Tyrfing

flesh rotting and bones showing, carrying a black leather saddle upon its back. The dark elf mounted and rode away through the trees.

Grimfar stood in silence, surveying the crumpled bodies around him.

A baby's soft whimper startled him.

"Baby still here?" he asked aloud.

Suddenly, as Grimfar strode toward the snow-covered tent, one of the barbarian skeletons began to rise unsteadily. Its bones creaked, the blood on them had already dried. Grimfar stopped. Raising his spear in front of him, the troll stepped forward and the skeleton stepped forward to meet him. Instantly, the troll dropped his spear and snatched his sword from the scabbard on his back. Slashing downward as he drew, Grimfar struck the skeleton in the chest and shattered it. Victorious, he sheathed his sword, picked up his spear and stepped over the pile it had left behind.

But the instant their comrade fell, three more skeletons rose up from the bloody snow. Grimfar took a small step back. One skeleton slashed its hunting knife at him. He dodged then pushed through the skeletons with his spear, smashing them as he pressed forward. But as he neared the center tent, he heard a dry rattle and knew that more skeletons had followed. He spun around and barely eluded a swinging halberd. Again, the skeleton swung its blade at him. He blocked and pushed back, but the creature swung the handle behind him, striking his calves and knocking him backward. The huge troll stumbled over the pile of bones behind him and fell to his back. A second skeleton raised its short sword high to drive it into the troll's chest.

Suddenly, a wolf leapt through the air and clamped its jaws down onto the skeleton's bony arm, ripping it off and shattering the skeleton with brute force. Grimfar was on his feet in a moment and looked around quickly. Wolves were leaping at the skeletons as soon as they could rise, tearing them to bits and strewing the bones around the camp. What manner of wolves were these that would protect something with meat on it and attack that without?

Grimfar soon found out, for the wolf who had saved his life turned toward him and transformed into an elf. They were druids, woodland elves able to assume the shape of wild animals. The elf was clothed in the furs of bears and wolves and his head was protected by the empty polished skull of a wolf.

"The child. Get the child." the elf said hastily, turned and became a wolf once again, lunging toward the animated dead. Grimfar turned and sped toward a nearby tent. He leaned his spear against the tent and looked inside. A makeshift crib lined with soft furs stood in one corner of the tent. Inside lay a baby, barely six months old, looking around with small blue eyes glistening with tiny baby tears. Grimfar gave a relieved sigh and stepped further inside.

By Sokarjo Stormwillow

Instantly a pitiful howl sprang into the darkening sky. "Grimfar take baby far 'way from evil bones. Grimfar tink dis not good place fer baby." The troll stepped quickly over to the crib as he spoke and lifted the child into his arms. Wrapping it in the furs, Grimfar bound the infant to his gator-armored chest with bands of leather. Outside the tent, Grimfar picked up his spear and fled quickly away from the camp. Behind him the druid wolves followed, leaving shattered piles of bones everywhere.

Soon after the unusual party fled the camp, more wolves rushed in. These wolves were not the disguised forms of elves, for their rotting flesh barely clung to their revealed bones, and their eyes were aglow with an evil red light.

Grimfar ran. Through the trees, over fallen logs, leaping at times over icy creeks the troll pounded through the snowy forests of Gamlin. Behind him raced the druids, their four-legged forms increasing their speed, their sides heaving and their paws barely touching the ground. Deeper and deeper into the pine woods they ran, knowing that the undead were giving chase and they must not abandon the troll or what he carried.

Suddenly, the cry of a wolf in pain echoed through the cedars. Grimfar spun around in his tracks and saw one wolf crashing into the underbrush. The troll rushed to the fallen druid's side. The elf had resumed his natural form as he fell, and his wolf-head helmet rolled off into the undergrowth as he landed on his stomach by a fallen log. His foot was caught in the iron teeth of a dwarven trap. Grimfar knelt by the elf's side and, growling with tremendous strength, pulled the trap open, setting the elf's foot free. The troll lifted him up, slung him over his massive shoulder and resumed his escape. But his burdens weakened him, slowing him down. Several times he stumbled, but always managed to catch himself and press on. His will was strong and his muscles strained.

Yet it was not enough. The pursuing undead were gaining ground quickly. Within moments they were on top of him. One leapt for his upper leg and sank its yellowed teeth deep into the sweaty muscle. Grimfar cried out, his pain-filled roar echoing through the forest.

Instantly, an illuminated arrow whizzed through the air, catching the evil creature in its throat. The undead wolf released its grip and fell, lifeless and inanimate, to the forest floor, crumbling into ash and dust. Seconds later, the air was filled with bright arrows striking down the vile creatures. Grimfar dropped to his knees, his face twisted in pain. Blood streamed down his leg and onto the dirty, snow-patched ground. But even through the extreme pain, the troll's will was strong. He held the wounded druid tightly with one hand and raised his spear to defend his burdens from their wicked pursuers.

The Tale of Tyrfing

Chapter Two

The dark elf and his decaying transport were plunging through the evergreens at breakneck speed. When a sudden pained cry erupted through the woods, he reined in the rotting animal and looked back toward the sound. An evil smile played about his swarthy lips and his dark eyes revealed grim satisfaction. He said not a word, but spurred his mount on, crashing through the forest. On and on he rode, far away from the snowy peaks and the fresh-smelling foliage of the mountains. The trees became thicker and the snow thinned then vanished entirely. The cedars and firs gave way to birch and oak. The snowy forests of Gamlin slowly became the dense beauty of the Entas Wood. Tall, majestic pines and green, flowery underbrush closely surrounded the elf of darkness as he rode relentlessly toward his destination. The chilly mountain air became a fresh, cool breeze and a light mist blanketed the ground beneath the ancient trees. These woods were filled with Entas, but the elf was not afraid of them; he knew they would flee his presence. Indeed, his influence upon living things was quite enough to make any shepherd of the forest hide. As he passed, each living thing near him began to wilt and die. The grass turned yellow then brown, the leaves curled up and withered, the flowers faded, and the branches drooped. Any Entas of sensible mind would have stayed far, far away from the drow's course that day. His power surged throughout his body, pounding through his veins and seething into his already shadowy soul.

Two nights passed and yet the bear did not slow his pace nor stop for sleep. He traveled on, relentless and unnaturally alert. Similarly, the elf himself did not seem to tire or desire rest. They continued on for some time and the forest began to diminish. The edge of the wood stopped suddenly, breaking like water upon rock into a vast expanse of plains grass and short, stubby bushes. The dark elf seemed content to be out of the magnificent forest, somewhat grateful for the hot, dry air and the lack of greenery. He had left the Entas Wood and was now traveling swiftly through the grasslands of the Helianto Plains. His path of death and destruction continued strong behind him, and he feared neither Gntahk nor beast.

Again, time passed. Several days had slowly rolled by, and yet the shadow elf did not stop for rest or food. He seemed driven by an unnatural hunger, a desire for power that removed from him all need for natural sustenance. Now he was surrounded by beautiful, rolling green hills and meadows full of exquisite flowers beckoned to all but him as they bathed in the warm afternoon sun. The trees were few in number, but grand and strong and large. He knew he had now entered Hakik, the land of the gnomes. His journey was drawing to a close.

A castle, towering high and menacing above the great trees around its black walls, called to him. "Master!" it gasped in a rasping voice only he could hear. He quickly answered its call and entered the castle's clearing. This was like no other clearing in the lands of Hakik, for within it nothing lived. Each blade of grass, each tree and leaf, each flower and weed was dead. Rocky dirt replaced the lush green turf; the empty branches stretched their black arms toward the darkening sky as if appealing to the heavens for aid. Even the rich brown soil was replaced with blackened sod, littered with ashes.

The dark elf dismounted his summoned convey. The bear hesitated a moment as the ground beneath him began to shift. A dozen skeletal arms reached up through the bubbling soil and commenced to rip off what was left of the bear's hide. Rotting flesh and dirty fur peeled away and vanished beneath the terrain. Soon all that was left were dried up bones. The bear's grotesque form reared onto its hind legs and roared hideously, falling backward onto the rocky ground. The bones crumbled and became dust, blowing away with the ashes on the evening breeze. The elf strode slowly forward, breathing in the soot-filled air and beholding his precious stronghold.

He stopped at the doorway and his sharp eyes noticed something. It was a weed, pitiful and thin, struggling to grow against the black stone walls of the fortress. He glared at it, then reached out and touched its feeble vines. The green plant wilted and died, the last remaining life on the cursed land surrounding the sinister castle. The dark elf turned and held up his hand. As if the large double doors had been awaiting the appearance of those long, slender fingers for years, they swung open, squeaking eerily on their rusted hinges. The drow entered and the doors slammed shut behind him, echoing through the dusky forest.

Somewhere that night, not too many miles away, a small band of men slept. They were new to these lands, but not unwelcome as the necromancer.

The Tale of Tyrfing

The gnomes had made certain of their comfort before snuffing their own lights, yet none of them slept deeply. Uneasiness spread through their small troop like a mist, hanging heavily upon them and shrouding their thoughts and dreams. Their skin was a deep bronze and their hair as dark ebony. They were clothed in soft silk, dyed vivid blues and greens and their long, gnarled staffs lay beside them on the dew soaked ground. They were mages, come from far away and seeking great knowledge from the scholars of the gnomish world. They were called Mazi, wise men from the land of Skarlein.

Suddenly, as the slamming of a door echoed through the woods, one of them sat up, looking around wildly. The sound pounded loudly in his head and he pondered fearfully what it could mean, though in his heart he knew it was the sound of a great evil. He picked up his staff from beside him and crept into the forest, careful not to awaken his companions.

The magician strolled through the trees, deep in thought and unable to sleep. The moon was dark, but the stars glowed brightly, lighting up the shadowy forest. A voice behind him startled him.

"Kwea?"

He did not turn, only stopped and said softly, "yes, Krimple?"

A small figure, barely twelve inches tall, scrambled up onto a nearby branch. The figure was aged and his long white beard was nearing his waist, but he was not stooped and had no difficulty walking along the narrow branch. He carried a staff, but it was merely for magical purposes, not for aid in walking. He was a gnome and, as old as he appeared, he was still quite young, for though he already had many grandchildren, his father, grandfather and even his great-grandfather, the king of the Bumblegorf gnomes, yet lived. He was a scholar mostly, but skilled in the art of elemental magic.

The gnome flopped down onto the branch, shaking it rather roughly and nearly losing his balance. He grinned sheepishly up at Kwea, but seeing the Mazi's somber face, quickly lost his cheer and became just as solemn.

"Kwea, my friend, what can ya be doin' out here? Should ya not be getting' some rest afore ya leave tomorrow? 'Tis a great way to your home in Skarlein."

"Yes, Krimple, but my dreams have become little more than nightmares and I find it rather difficult to slumber." Kwea sat down against a nearby tree. "Would you grace me with a gnomish tune, my friend?"

"I would be honored to."

The gnome leapt to his feet atop his perilous perch and began to sing. His melodious voice echoed through the trees, the beautiful music carried on the cool night breeze to far away places. The words themselves were of an ancient language, unspoken now by any tongue but the gnomes.

By Sokarjo Stormwillow

The copper-toned man closed his dark, weary eyes and a small, tender smile played about his lips. His tense muscles began to slowly relax and he rested his head against the tree. Soon the soft notes filled his somnolent mind and he drifted off into a restful sleep.

As the Mazi slumbered, the gnome's refrain echoed throughout the wooded hills. The lovely music floated on the midnight wind, drifting through the trees and alighting on the welcoming ears of the woodland inhabitants.

That is, until it fell upon those of a necromantic elf.

"Intolerable gnomes!" the shadow elf muttered. Standing on a balcony high upon the onyx walls of his bleak castle, the elf glared angrily into the moonless darkness. He turned away and strode quickly into the castle, slamming the great doors behind him. The music was immediately cut off from him and the elf turned to face a dark corner, motioning with his hands. "Bring me your pitiful excuse for a leader!" A goblin screeched and scrambled away, nearly tripping over its own feet. The necromancer smiled grimly in pleasure at the creature's fear.

Moments later, a goblin, cloaked in torn leather and chain mail, crept nervously through the large double doors. The necromancer was seated at the head of a long table lit only by two weak candles. The flickering light cast menacing shadows on his face, striking even more fear into the heart of an already terrified goblin.

"You... you wanted to see me, my lord?" The goblin asked in his deep, raspy voice.

"Stop sputtering, you fool!" The elf rose from his seat in anger. "I thought I gave specific instructions before I left. I do not want that party of Mazi leaving this wood! Destroy them! Tonight!"

"Y-Yes, my lord! I will!"

"See that you do, Krage." The elf commanded, lowering his voice to a menacing pitch. At the snap of the elf's slender fingers, a cage lowered onto the table. Trapped inside were seven goblins, clawing at the bars and screeching in terror. The goblin's eyes widened. "If you should fail me again, your head and theirs shall make the perfect ornaments for my castle grounds. GO!"

The goblin scrambled from the room to summon his army. In mere moments the night air was filled with the stench of decaying flesh as dozens of goblins sped from the castle grounds on the backs of undead wolves.

After the door had closed behind the goblin leader, the shadow elf looked menacingly at the cage of frightened goblins before him. "Bring me an axe," he ordered.

"Bu-but, my lord... Krage has only just left. He is sure to--" stammered a nearby goblin.

"Silence! Do not question me, worm!" the shadow elf raged, rising once more from his seat. Quieting his voice once more, speaking almost more to himself than the trembling goblin staring at him, he added, "Krage will fail me again." He slowly resumed his seat, staring intently at the shocked and shaking goblins caged before him. "His chances against the Mazi were nothing to begin with. No, his attack will merely lead them here.... where I will fight the mages on my own ground, where my power is strongest."

Krimple's song had ended and the mage slept peacefully. The gnome turned and hopped from branch to branch until he reached the ground near the Mazi's sleeping form. He began to walk softly away, then froze. Beneath his tiny feet he could feel the ground rumble softly. He knelt and pressed his ear against the grassy soil. His eyes widened and he leapt to his feet. Rushing over to the sleeping magician, Krimple began frantically shaking his hand.

"Wake up, Kwea! Come, friend! Wake up!" The Mazi slept peacefully on. "That's the last time I sing for you... you... oh, bumblesticks!" Frustrated, the gnome stepped back. He clapped his hands and the tree reached down a leafy bough, caught the Mazi up and shook him furiously. When Kwea began to yell, Krimple clapped his hands again. The tree dropped the mage to the ground and returned to its normal stance.

"You presumptuous gnome! Why, I should...." the Mazi began, angered by this rude awakening.

"Thank me! There be somethin' approachin' and 'tisn't peaceful!" Krimple stated in his defense.

Kwea closed his eyes and tilted his head downward, his brow furrowed as in distress. Krimple stood at his feet waiting anxiously. After a few seconds of silence, the mage lifted his head and opened his eyes slowly.

"It is as I feared. A great Evil is stirring. His minions come even now."

"Aye, now tell me somethin' I don't know!" Krimple cried in frustration.

Kwea ignored his comment. "Quickly, my friend. We must warn my brethren!"

Krimple could not hope to match the magician's long strides. He raised his hands and a fallen branch before him rose and began to shift. In no time at all, a bark-covered stallion of his size had risen from the ground and carried the gnome quickly toward his destination.

Mere seconds away, the goblin raiders were crashing through the woods, destroying everything in their path as they raced to obey their master's bidding. Even the very panting of their haunted mounts seemed to be murmuring 'death, death, death'. The trail they left behind them was not of lifeless forest such as the drow had left, but the destruction was nearly as terrible; broken trees, crushed flowers, slashed bushes and wounded creatures. The leader raised his hand and the entire party came to a sudden halt. Only a few trees separated them from the Mazi camp. Large, lumpy bedrolls were clustered around a small crackling fire.

"We must attack now, while the mages sleep. We stand a better chance for victory," was the growled suggestion to the leader. The grim captain turned to glare at his bold advisor, but did not scold him. Instead he looked forward and gave his command. When he spoke, his voice was quiet, but full of hatred. "Victory must be ours. Kill them!"

At the sound of this favored word, the goblin ranks plunged into the camp, screeching their war cry. The leader hung back, sulking in the woods, seemingly unsure whether to follow his raiders. The goblins tore madly at the blankets, making enough noise to be heard many miles away. One looked up wildly.

"Leaves!" he screeched in dismay and anger.

As if that had been their cue, dozens of Mazi surrounded the camp, instantly trapping the confused goblins. One of them stepped forward and spoke. "It seems the tables have been turned, vermin."

A few feet away, the goblin leader could only watch in alarm as the mages destroyed what was left of his meager army using fire, water, wind, ice and lightning. He stumbled back a couple steps and tripped on a branch lying behind him. In an instant, the branch came to life, wrapping itself around his legs and pinning him to the ground, cutting off any hopes he may have had of escape.

"Ya won't be gettin' away this time, monster!" a tiny man yelled at him. A Mazi stepped up and pointed his staff at the goblin's feet. Instantly, the branch froze to the ground, clutching the goblin in an icy firm grip.

"Tell us, death chaser. Who has sent you?" Kwea asked, staring intently into the eyes of the goblin. "Come on, you. Speak up!"

"I am Krage. I will tell you who seeks to destroy you. But in return, I ask a favor." the goblin snarled.

The Mazi and gnome shared annoyed glances. "And ya shall get one," the gnome replied, with a nod. "Your life! Now answer us!"

"Please," the goblin's voice softened, almost too soft for a creature such as he was. "I ask only that you rescue my brothers."

Surprised, the Mazi looked at him questioningly. "You are an unusual goblin. What should you care if your men die?"

"Those goblins out there?" Krage scoffed, motioning to the last remaining raiders in the camp. "I don't. You are correct when you say I am no ordinary goblin. At a time long since past, I was not a goblin, but a man. A human from the land of Damor. I surprise you. Of course. I no longer hold resemblance to my former self." the goblin's voice was raspy and sinister as all goblins' should be, but there was a strange calmness and he spoke with more intelligence than any common goblin could.

"I am interested in hearing how you became a goblin. That is no ordinary transition," Kwea responded, skeptically.

"No it is not," the goblin groaned. His face twisted in a mixture of pain, anger and sadness as he remembered his past. "My memories are clouded, mostly in pain. I was once a great leader among my tribe. Then He deceived me. He promised me power beyond imagination. What I got was torture and mutilation." The word came out with a throaty, animalistic growl. "He is the one who made me into this... this creature. But He didn't stop there. He forced me to watch as He murdered my mother, my father, my sisters-- and my beautiful bride. All He left to me were my brothers, tortured and deformed beyond any recognition. They are at His castle now. And if I do not return victorious, they will lose their heads."

"Who is he? Who is this demon you speak of?" Kwea asked, suddenly filled with indignation as he began to believe this tormented being.

"His name.... is Nakasuin."

Chapter Three

Year 16 of the Divided Age, TThe Lost Continent of Piyr
Midgard

A small group of lively young children ran through the grasses in front of the old hut, chasing one another and laughing with glee. A small, shaggy dog ran behind them, nipping playfully at their heels. A woman, aged and graying, sat near the doorway of the cottage, churning butter and watching the children's antics with a smile playing about her dry, cracked lips. The sun beat down upon her and the wind blew her tattered shawl off of her head and onto her shoulders, allowing the hot rays to strike her wrinkled face. Her ragged brown dress whipped about her bare feet and her hair was beginning to come out of its salt-and-pepper bun. All this she ignored, paying attention only partially to the butter, and primarily to the children playing before her.

Presently, a younger woman with a beautiful, anguished face stepped out of the hut, her equally ragged blue gown caught suddenly by the wind. She raised a shaking hand to brush back the long sunny locks that the wind blew into her face. In her other arm she held a small baby boy, whose plump cheeks were rosy and whose sparkling eyes watched the other children at play.

"My dear Traida, why do you shiver so?" the older woman asked. "Are you ill?"

"Not ill, mother; afraid. It has been six years since we came here, and I still fear. I will not be comforted until Jaykon rides up over that hill once more and I know that he... that we all are safe." the younger woman answered, her eyes searching a nearby hilltop.

"I understand your fear, daughter." the old woman's voice was soft, gentle and comforting. "Perhaps Jaykon will return and tell us that we are safe here forever. Perhaps we will not have to run again. But for now, we must gain strength from each other and above all, we must not let the children see our fear."

"Yes, mother. I know. I am trying. It is... difficult." The woman sighed and turned to enter the house once again.

Suddenly a triumphant cry went up from the children. "Papa's home! Papa's home!" and they rushed toward a mounted figure descending the nearest hill. The woman spun around, her face a mixture of hope and uncertainty. Quickly she set the baby on the ground beside the old woman and stepped forward, her hand on her breast to still her racing heart.

The older woman rose from her task and stepped to her daughter's side. "You see, Traida. All shall be well with us, if we hold faith." Traida did not respond, but the look on her face showed her feelings clearly.

The man spurred his horse and galloped toward them. As he neared, they could see the joy and longing in his face. 'Home'... the word rang in his head. That was what he hoped for. Dismounting his steed, he dropped the reigns as all five of his children crowded around him, begging for attention and nearly knocking him over. He laughed and picked up the little girl, lifting her into the air and spinning her around. Her golden curls bounced up and down on her rosy cheeks and her eyes sparkled as her brothers clamored for their turn in papa's arms. Finally, he looked up, his eyes rested on the fair face of his wife and he set his children down and strode quickly toward her. She could not wait. Bounding down the path like a child, she sprang into his arms, gripping him tightly as he returned her embrace.

"I am home, my love, my dear," he said. He held her at arm's length and gazed lovingly into her lovely grey eyes then, overcome by his emotions, he kissed her passionately. The children giggled and the old woman smiled so broadly, she thought her face would burst.

Finally, the man looked up at the elderly woman and smiled. "G'day, dear Gemaine! Will we be having some of your heavenly bread tonight?"

"Of course, Jaykon." Gemaine said, smiling back, accepting his embrace as if he were her son. "It's in the oven right now, and the butter is just ready. Go inside, you must be exhausted."

Traida lifted the toddler into her arms and led her husband past her grinning mother and into their humble abode. The children followed after and Gemaine turned to bring in her churner. Before she could lift it up, Jaykon quickly returned and snatched it from her.

"You just get on inside yourself, Gemaine. I have this." Gemaine followed Jaykon into the hut with a grateful smile.

The eldest boy, a strapping lad of fifteen, took his father's horse and led him to the corral behind the house. The horses whimpered as he removed the saddle and closed the gate. The cows grumbled in the barn and the chickens chattered amongst themselves. There was an uneasy stir amid the

The Tale of Tyrfing

animals that their owners did not see. Had they noticed, they might have been more prepared for what was to happen that night.

The table was laid in festivity for the return of the man of the house. Traida had cleaned the house twice and placed fresh flowers upon the table and Gemaine had prepared a luscious supper, fit for a king: soft bread, succulent boar steaks, steaming vegetables, ripe tomatoes, golden butter, creamy milk and a mug of ale for Jaykon. A dessert of warm apple pie and smooth, sweet cream, beckoned to them from the kitchen as they sat down to enjoy their delicious meal.

When the feast was over, the youngest boys gathered round their father and Traida sat next to him, her arm in his as he began to tell his stories, baby Keenan on his lap. Aelfric, a ruddy-haired, freckle-faced boy of three, sat on the floor before his father, flanked on either side by his two-year old twin brothers, Conary and Elwen. Gemaine and the two eldest children, the golden haired girl and her sulking brother, joined Gemaine in the kitchen to wash up the dishes. Little Colly dried the dishes and leaned close the crack in the door, trying to catch bits of her father's tale.

"Come on, Colly!" Her brother said impatiently. "If you'd work faster, we could go out and hear it all!"

"But, Seaghan, we're missing the best part! Oh, Grandmamma! Why can't we do the dishes after Father tells his story?"

"Because, my dear, you always fall asleep before he's done. I can't do it all by myself, now can I?" Gemaine smiled at her granddaughter and handed her a dry towel. "Here, yours is too wet."

Colly took the towel and began drying the dishes as fast as her little six-year old hands would let her.

"Colly, you'd best be careful..." Seaghan began to warn her as he poked more logs into the stove.

"Hush!" Gemaine exclaimed. The children froze.

Outside, they heard horses' hooves, pounding the hard ground.

"Seaghan," Gemaine whispered. "Quickly, hide with your sister in the potato bin." Seaghan nodded and swept his sister into the giant bin. Gemaine closed the lid and set a barrel of apples on top. Turning, she snatched up a butcher knife and brandished it, facing the door.

In the front room, the storytelling had stopped. The horses had stopped outside the front door and the house fell silent. Suddenly, someone pounded loudly on the door. Keenan whimpered. Jaykon set the toddler on his mother's lap and stepped to the door, pulling his sword from its sheath. Looking back, he motioned for silence.

"Who knocks on my door at this time of night?" Jaykon called with his sword brandished and ready.

"Open up in the name of King Kermain!" a loud, gruff voice answered.

Jaykon's face blanched white. Traida clutched her child in her arms, her eyes showing sheer terror. The other three drew close to her, clinging to her skirts and watching their father closely. Jaykon took a breath and shot a painful look at his beloved family. Traida's face became calm and she nodded in understanding to her husband.

"Kermain is not a king, but a murderer and a traitor! I will not open up to you!" Jaykon declared, turning towards the door and gripping his sword tightly. Instantly, the door was kicked down and a broad-shouldered brute of a man strode through the broken doorway. Within moments he had relieved Jaykon of his sword. Jaykon was knocked to the floor, his meager sword broken and tossed into a corner. The man before him leaned a scarred face down close and grinned, his foul breath churning Jaykon's stomach.

"You should have kept practicing with that toy-- brother." The man spat the word out as if it were poison.

Seaghan was barely able to stifle Colly's cries as the death-screams of their family broke the stillness of the night. Gemaine's face streamed wet with tears of anger, fear and loss. Her daughter was dying, with her husband and children, and there was nothing an old woman could do. Her heart broke with each second, as she heard the pleas of her grandchildren and their parents. Tears streamed down her face as she remembered the six of them, running and laughing in front of the hut only hours before. Now, only two remained and her heart begged for their lives to be spared.

The house was silent. Silent as the grave, Gemaine thought. Silence passed for a moment, then a gruff voice addressed the leader. "They're all dead, my lord."

She heard a man walk heavily towards the kitchen. Her heart pounded loudly in her ears and her withered hand gripped the large knife more tightly. She stood braced and ready to defend her surviving grandchildren with every ounce of strength she had left, though she knew it was little.

"Where do you think you're going?" the leader demanded.

"To get some grub! I'm starving," the man said angrily, his voice coming dangerously close to the kitchen door. "Killing is hungry business."

"No! Never eat the food from a house of blood. We have slain the inhabitants, now the food is cursed to us. Come! We leave immediately." Gemaine closed her eyes and sighed softly in relief as the heavy footsteps of the men retreated and left the house.

After the horses rode away, Gemaine dropped the knife onto the floor, one hand to her heart, the other supporting her weary weight on the table.

Blood was trickling into the kitchen from beneath the half shut door and Gemaine cringed as she thought of the loved ones whose blood was smeared across the floor. Her heart rejoiced as she heard Colly's stifled sobs. Thank the Gods that Seaghan was able to keep her quiet until the men left.

"Stay there, my dears," she begged in a teary whisper. She stepped toward the front room door which was still slightly ajar. Blood was splattered everywhere and her family's bodies lay scattered across the room. Gemaine brushed away tears as a sob caught in her throat, and softly closed the door. There was no need for the children to see that. Their dreams would be nightmares enough from just the screams. They did not need to see the carnage as well.

Gemaine moved quickly and with purpose. Someone was bound to come, to see what had happened. They could not be found here. No one knew how many lived here, not even Kermain. If he found out about Seaghan and Colly, they too would die. She had to get them as far away as possible, and quickly. She silently prayed that her own son, Gren, who lived alone nearby, would escape the bloodthirsty riders.

She snatched a satchel from a hook beside the firebox. The last of the bread, some raisins and nuts, and a few biscuits only filled the sack halfway. She didn't want it too heavy, but added some apples, potatoes, cheese, and dried beans. To this she also added a small pot, a kettle, some flint, then tied the bag shut with a bit of rope. Before calling the children out, Gemaine took the rug from in front of the washtub and tossed it by the door to cover the dark puddle of blood forming.

"Seaghan. Colly. Come out quickly, children. We must go now." Gemaine said, lifting the barrel off of the bin and removing the lid.

"Where are we going, Grandmother?" Seaghan asked as he helped his little sister out of their hiding place. Their faces were soaked with tears, Colly's little lips still quivering, yet Seaghan bravely kept his voice firm.

"Far away from here, dear. Come quickly. We leave through the window." She had to keep them out of the living room.

Seaghan understood, wiped his cheek with his arm, and lifted his sister up, handing her to Gemaine who had already climbed through the window. Seaghan glanced behind him at the closed door then followed his little sister through the window.

The children quickly found their beloved white dog and began petting and cuddling it.

"Good old Freeno," Gemaine sighed, smiling. "I am glad you made it alright." As she said this, she took a piece of red cord from a nearby worktable and handed it to Seaghan. "Here, put this on him. We must be sure he stays quiet and close to us. For now at least."

Seaghan took the rope and tied it around the pup's neck. Gemaine picked up a small hatchet and placed it into the bag she carried then looked around. "No other animals," she observed. "Kermain and his men must have taken them. Well, my dears. We shall have to walk. The horses are gone too, I imagine."

And they were. There was no sign of them anywhere. "Well, we shall have to walk, then." Gemaine took her staff from beside the barn door and set out in an easterly direction. On a sudden impulse she stopped, turned and snatched up her two remaining grandchildren into her arms. Holding them tightly, she murmured, "Twill be alright, dears. We can make it together. We still have each other at least." Seaghan, with his steely green eyes so much like his father's, and Colly, with tears in her soft blue eyes, looked up at their grandmother.

"Yes, Grandmother." Seaghan said, quietly. "We will be alright. I'll make sure of that."

Gemaine kissed them both on their cheeks and foreheads, hugged them once more, then rose and they walked off, side by side. Colly clutched Gemaine's hand and Seaghan led Freeno as they approached a dark forest. I'll make sure of it; he repeated to himself and gripped the dog's cord even tighter.

Chapter Four

The stars glistened in the ebony sky and the wind howled woefully through the pines. The elderly dwarf shivered as chills crept down his back. Being a dwarf, he was very much accustomed to the chilly mountain air and the dark shadows. But tonight was different. Tonight, he felt an evil lurking somewhere, out there in the darkness of Gamlin, and the hair on his back crawled with fear. There were no cheerful chirps from the crickets and the night birds were silent as well.

The short, stocky, grey-bearded man looked up at his companion. A stranger he was: tall, dark and mysterious, like the woods around them. A ragged deep green cloak, muddied on the bottom, shrouded his body, hiding most of his facial features. But the dwarf had seen them well enough before. He was an elderly man, a wizard from Golondere. White hair draped over his shoulders and a beard just as long, though thinner than the dwarf's, rested on his chest. Piercing brown eyes took the courage from even those who had much to spare, and searched their very souls. The dwarf recalled the moment, only a few hours behind him, when the wizard had introduced himself.

A brilliant red-hot fire had been crackling in the fireplace, and flaming raw meat sizzled on the spit. Oh, what he wouldn't give for a huge chunk of that juicy steak right now. He remembered the pungent odors, the succulent flavors, and the delicious juices that ran down his beard. He thought longingly of the strong ales and pictured the table, laid with all manner of scrumptious victuals. How he wished he were back home in the warm caves of his fellow dwarves!

Galen, a lookout, had come in and announced that a rather large man was outside, and he was looking for the lord of the mountain. That was who this elderly dwarf was: Kundin, Lord of Mount Roguk, and leader of the Kaladure Clan hidden deep beneath its stony heights.

By Sokarjo Stormwillow

The lofty gentleman had swept into the dining hall, bringing with him an icy breeze from the mountains. Snow topped his pointed green hat and brushed across his shoulders and his boots. His bright red nose, glowing from the frigid air, was really the only bright thing about him. His very presence in the great dining hall had brought apprehension to the heart of many a brave dwarf. Quiet whispers floated about the room; murmurs of what a man like him could possibly want in Gamlin, and even more so, in Mount Roguk. He strode forward swiftly until he reached the table of the lord of the mountain. He clutched in his hand a staff, carved out of a mighty oak, holding in its tip, an ancient white stone. The wizard had stood quiet for a moment and the entire room fell utterly silent.

Finally, slightly annoyed by the extended silence of the great man, Kundin had asked, "Who are you, good sir? And what business do you have with me?"

The wizard then spoke and all eyes were fixed upon him as he did.

"I am Berinder, from the realm of Golondere. Kundin, son of Bali, I come to you... with a story." Confused looks had swept about the room as the wizard took a seat. This formidable wizard had barged into the dining halls of a dwarven lord and demanded to tell him a story? But none breathed a word against him and instead listened intently.

The wizard began in a great booming voice which filled the hall and echoed off the stone walls. "Hundreds of years ago, a king named Svafurlami, went hunting in the mountains of Gamlin. He became separated from his hunting party and was quite alone. But he knew no fear and continued his hunt. After some time, he spotted a magnificent white stag grazing in a meadow. Svafurlami gave chase, but eventually lost his quarry. The man cared not, however, for he had spied two dwarves, Durrin and Dvalin by name. These two dwarves were well known for their abilities in the forging of magical weaponry. He took them by surprise, demanding that they fashion for him, a sword of fantastic power. This sword should never become dull, and should cut through stone and iron as if through cloth. It should also bring its bearer victory in every battle. The dwarves agreed and scurried into their small cave within the rocks to forge this mighty sword. The dark king of Damor sat and waited beneath a tree. Just before dawn, the dwarves emerged, bearing a broadsword of great magnificence. Its scabbard was golden and on it was depicted the deeds of the ancient gods. Guard, grip and pommel were of gold as well, studded with many fine jewels. Svafurlami grasped the sword and when he drew it, he saw that the steel was flawless."

Every dwarf in the great hall had sat silent, listening intently to the stranger's story. But Kundin immediately cut in.

The Tale of Tyrfing

"Aye, wizard. The sword was indeed a masterpiece. I know this tale. I heard it many times from my grandfather when I was a youngling." The wizard nodded and swept his hand, beckoning for Kundin to finish the story. The dwarves turned inquisitive looks toward Kundin. He paused for a moment then picked up where the wizard had been interrupted.

"Durrin and Dvalin, two of the greatest of our mighty race..." at this the wizard seemed to show a hint of a smile, but it was fleeting. "...made a mockery of this king of men. To his three requirements, they added four more. The first, my good wizard, was that no wound made by it could be healed. The second: once it was drawn from the scabbard, it must shed human blood before it can be sheathed again. Thirdly, three deeds of woe should be wrought with it. And finally, they added that Svafurlami himself would die by its flawless blade. In anger, he struck at them, but they escaped and returned to their halls in the mountain. The sword's name was Tyrfing, lord wizard, and the dwarves, Durrin and Dvalin, are ancestors of my clan, the Kaladure. Svafurlami was victorious and destroyed many men and armies. But indeed, the sword did kill him. His pride led him to do battle in the Helianto Plains with a raider from Kerik. Svafurlami swung at the raider and missed, burying Tyrfing in the soil. Pulling the sword free, the raider hewed Svafurlami to the ground. He then took the sword and kept it. The raider's daughter claimed Tyrfing, giving it to her son, who killed his brother with it. As its third act of bloodshed, Tyrfing was used by thralls to kill this son in the night. Thus, having shed its appointed amount of blood, the legendary sword, Tyrfing, vanished from the chronicles of Midgard and has become nothing more than a legend." This last was spoken in casual disbelief.

"Until now, Lord Kundin," the wizard boomed. "Tyrfing is once more a threat to Piyr. It has been found and is in the possession of a mighty foe. This foe will not use it himself, but the only living descendant of Svafurlami is searching for the blade, and if he finds it, it will be the end of our world as we know it. This weapon must be destroyed!"

"But Svafurlami had no living descendants! They were all destroyed by the same man who killed him," Kundin exclaimed, astonished. "It's impossible!"

"Nay, master dwarf, it is very much true. A soldier escaped with a small baby. That child grew to reclaim the lands of his father, and his great-grandson, Tahlon, the last High King of Damor, was murdered by his own son sixteen years ago this day, an act beginning the years of the Divided Age of Man. And I have just received word that this same murderous son has killed his younger brother and his entire family. The son, Kermain, had been disowned, so his younger brother was in line for the throne. However, now that there is no other living relative, it will be much easier for Kermain to claim that right."

"What has this to do with me or my clan? Or even Tyrfing?" Kundin was impatient. He cared not for the troubles of men. They were a foolish race and he preferred to concern himself only with the well being of his own kin.

"Because you are the direct descendant of those who constructed Tyrfing, therefore you are the only one who can destroy it!" the wizard rose in controlled fury. "If this murderer gets his hands on this sword of death, do not think he will stop with the race of men, nor the people of Damor. Long has he desired the great wealth in the mines of Gamlin, and with Tyrfing in his hands, there are none will stop him!"

The wizard snatched up his staff and placed his hat upon his head once again. "I leave now, for the island of Élas, beyond the Theilas Ocean, where the elfin lord, Almyn Ostara dwells. He has offered to aid us in our quest to destroy this evil. Will you join me or not? The fate of Midgard as we know it rests in your hands, master dwarf. What is your decision?"

He had come, of course. Who could say no to that? He had left his trusted friend, Thlungmal, in charge and he had come. Now he was wondering if it had been such a wise choice. He was hungry, cold and exhausted. It was difficult for a dwarf of his age to keep up with such a long-legged fellow, his legs being short as they were. But he dared not complain. Berinder was not to be trifled with. Besides, it would make him look weak and that was unfitting for a dwarven lord. So he pressed on, warily keeping an eye on the dark trees and shifting shadows.

Suddenly, the wizard spoke, startling Kundin. "We are nearing the Entas Wood, master dwarf. Keep a sharp eye. Many dangers yet lurk within these ancient woods. We shall spend as little time in the forest as possible."

"Why are we heading this way at all? Why did we not just go west from Mount Roguk to Tobli? This is a rather long way to Élas, is it not?"

"In due time, Lord Kundin, in due time. First we must meet a friend of mine in Kerik."

The Tale of Tyrfing

Chapter Five

The sun gleamed across rolling fields of ripened wheat, swaying in the gentle breeze that whispered through small scatterings of oak and hickory. Birds whistled merrily to each other and darted about, searching for wriggling worms in the late morning's warmth. Rabbits zigzagged through the fields, occasionally darting out in front of the group of travelers and exciting their canine companion.

Seaghan followed Gemaine, lost in thought. He tried hard, he really did. But it was too soon, too fresh in his mind. He remembered the chilling screams, the evil laughter, the terrified gripping in his chest, the fatal horror of that night. It had been nine days since they had fled in terror from the hut in which his family's lives had ended so abruptly, but he relived those horrid moments over and over. He fought against the memories, but lost every battle. His heart pounded and his steps became less stable as his mind drew near once again, to the moment the monster had slammed through the door.

Suddenly, his nightmarish thoughts were interrupted by a sharp yank on the cord tied round his hand.

"Freeno, come on!" he growled. "Do you have to sniff every single tree?" He jerked the cord impatiently, pulling the curious mutt along.

Gemaine looked over her shoulder at the boy and smiled sadly. "So young," she thought to herself. "So young to have lost so much."

They trudged on in silence, stopping every so often so the old lady could rest.

After some time, Freeno began acting strange. He became easily frightened and seemed to jump at every sound. After the third or fourth instance, Seaghan became annoyed and grumbled at the dog. "Come on! What's wrong with you, boy?" A moment later, Seaghan let out another "Come on!" and yanked the dog's cord. Gemaine glanced back at Freeno, a concerned look upon her face. The mutt looked up at her and whimpered. The elderly woman stopped and looked around. The sun was high in the sky and there was a slight breeze. She listened closely as the children watched her with frightened eyes.

"Grandmamma?" Colly asked clutching tightly to Gemaine's wrinkled hand. "What's wrong?"

"Hush, child. I'm listening."

A strained pause.

"For what, Grandmamma?" Colly whispered, rather loudly.

"I don't know yet."

Suddenly she heard it. The bark of a warg, followed by a most horrific screech.

"Goblins!" she gasped. "Run!"

She didn't have to say it again. The children had never encountered goblins before, but they had heard many a gruesome tale and knew they were in grave danger. Freeno was grateful for the chance to run and the four of them scrambled through tall grasses and over fallen logs as fast as they could. But two children and an old lady are rather slow, especially in unfamiliar land. Behind them, the screeches became louder as the warg riders drew ever closer.

Suddenly, Colly tripped and fell and Gemaine spun round to lift her up. She had caught her ankle in a tree root. Seaghan dropped to his knees beside his small sister as Gemaine tried to pull her free, but to no avail. Even removing Colly's black lace-up boot did not help. Seaghan began to panic.

"Grandmother! Get her out! Get her out!" he begged, nearly in tears.

Gemaine struggled with the root, then pulled out a small dagger and began hacking at it. But the root was strong and her dull blade had little effect. Her heart pounded in fear. She could not lose them! They had come this far, what could she do?

She looked up. The wargs and their sinister riders were close now, close enough to see and smell. Gemaine grasped a large branch and stepped in front of the children. She said nothing, but held her branch tightly and stood ready. Seaghan clutched his sister tightly as she sobbed, and struggled to get her ankle free.

Suddenly, a huge figure leapt in front of Gemaine, facing the goblins and brandishing a giant club. He was taller than a tall man, built like a giant and clothed like a barbarian. Gemaine stepped back, frightened but curious. Could it be that this was Thor, come to rescue them?

With amazing strength and force, the giant swung his club right and left, tossing the goblins aside and crushing their bodies. Even the vicious wargs

The Tale of Tyrfing

were no match for the brute. Within mere moments the entire goblin party was destroyed. Gemaine dropped the branch she still held and looked back at the children, relief flooding over her. Their rescuer turned to face them, lowering his club.

Gemaine gasped and stepped back as she laid eyes on his most dreadful face. This was certainly not the great Thunder God. His skin was emerald, sharp teeth protruded from his mouth and his visage was no less than terrifying. Gemaine knew this to be a troll, but he looked strangely different from the trolls she had seen in Berea as a young girl.

"Please sir," she begged. "Please have mercy on us." She clasped her hands together and dropped to her knees before him, her eyes meeting his. Seaghan and Colly did not move nor make a sound, but kept their eyes riveted on the creature. The brute, seemingly oblivious to the young ones, reached down and grasped Gemaine's arms, lifting her to her feet. Freeno stood nearby, wagging his tail and appearing to even smile.

When the troll spoke, his voice was deep and gruff, but his eyes sparkled. "I will not hurt you, little woman. I already had breakfast." And with that, the troll gave Gemaine a huge, ridiculous grin. Gemaine smiled weakly back, still a little unsure of this unusual troll.

Seaghan spoke softly and nervously. "Please, sir. She's stuck." Colly sat motionless as the troll stepped forward, grasped the root and lifted it up. Seaghan pulled his sister away from it and the troll set it gently back down, scooping earth over it to cover it completely.

Colly tried to stand, but whimpered and dropped back to the ground. Gemaine knelt beside her, concerned. "What is it, child?"

"My ankle. It hurts, Grandmamma," the girl replied, sniffling. The huge troll lifted her up in his arms as gently as a shepherd lifts a lamb.

"Mushbahc will carry the little girl. You must tell him where he's going though."

Gemaine nodded slowly. "We were on our way to the city of Cherin, in Damor."

Mushbahc turned and strode northwest, leading them on. Seaghan and Gemaine followed. Curious, Seaghan looked at Gemaine. "Damor, Grandmother?"

"Yes, Seaghan. To the palace of the king."

"Why are we going there?"

Gemaine smiled at him. "Because, my child. That is where your father is from."

Hours later, Gemaine, Seaghan, and Colly sat beneath a tree as Mushbahc left to scout the nearby woods. Gemaine tore strips of her skirt and began to bind Colly's ankle while Seaghan watched thoughtfully.

"Grandmother," he said, finally. "I want to know."

"Know what, child?"

"Everything. About my father. Who it is we fear. I want to know everything."

The old lady was quiet for a moment as she carefully tied a knot in the cloth around Colly's ankle. Finally she spoke.

"Yes, Seaghan. It is time you heard the truth. You should have been told years ago." She leaned back against the trunk of the tree and closed her eyes. After a short pause, she began.

"Years ago, in West Damor, Tahlon Jordahn sired two sons. The eldest was Kermain and the youngest was named Jaykon."

"Father?" Seaghan asked.

Gemaine opened her eyes and smiled faintly. "Yes, your father. The two lads never got along. Kermain was violent and angry and Jaykon was gentle and kind. It was as if they were from two different worlds. One day, when the two were young men, Kermain attacked Jaykon. He would have killed him, but a man by the name of Kilme rescued Jaykon and Kermain was banished from Damor for the attack on his brother. Bitter and angry, Kermain fled to the mountains of Gamlin. Damor was a peaceful place for a few years, until one night when Kermain returned to end Kilme's life. Tahlon attacked Kermain to protect his best friend and was hewn down by his own son. Kermain escaped with his life, but bore a scar upon his face, a gift from Kilme. Guards rushed in, but it was too late. Damor's king was dead."

"King?!?!" Seaghan exclaimed.

"Yes, Tahlon Jordahn, your grandfather, was the king of all Damor. In those days, the land was united under one ruler. But when Tahlon died, Damor split, the Western half ruled by faithful Kilme, the Eastern half by a greedy Duke. Jaykon fled from Cherin, disguised as a rogue. He had met a young girl on one of his travels to Kerik and had fallen in love with her. He sought her out, married her and changed his name to Brennan, hoping to live a peaceful peasant's life, unnoticed by his brother. But it was not to be."

Seaghan looked pale. "That man..." he said softly. "Was my uncle..."

"Yes, child. He has taken many innocent lives, and that is why we run."

Seaghan looked up at her. "Why are we going to Damor? Won't he find us there?"

"We will be safe under the protection of the new king. Kilme has only taken the throne until the rightful heir can be found."

"Father?" Colly asked.

"No. Seaghan."

Seaghan stared at her, speechless. "My brother's a king!" Colly exclaimed, giggling.

"Yes," Gemaine nodded. "Kermain was banished and disowned. Jaykon gave up the crown. The kingship falls to his eldest and now only remaining son."

All was quiet for several moments as Seaghan let the shocking truth sink in. Then he spoke.

"But, Grandmother. I can't be a king. I am just a boy."

"My son, you have spirit and strength. I am certain you can become the kind of king your grandfather was."

"How can I be great? I am just a.... a peasant."

"My dear, dear boy," Gemaine answered, smiling. "It is not who a man's father is, nor what a man's name is that makes him great. It is not even his position in life that makes him a king among men. Decisions, Seaghan. Consider your paths carefully. It is your heart and your faith that will make you great."

"But faith in what, Grandmother?"

"Faith in yourself... faith in the land... faith in the powers that protect them both."

"Will I know when I have become great enough?"

Gemaine smiled. "No, my child. It is when men know they are great, that they cease to be so. That knowledge only makes them dangerous."

Dangerous. That word held new meaning for Seaghan as scenes from the night his family died, flashed through his head. "I fear my uncle. I cannot be a king and feel fear, can I?"

"Yes, Seaghan. It is good for men to feel fear. It teaches them courage."

"But I thought courage was not being afraid."

A deep voice spoke before Gemaine could answer. "No, boy. Courage is to know what you fear... and to face it."

Seaghan looked down thoughtfully. "We must go now," Mushbahc said, lifting Colly up in his arms. "Goblins will search for the missing ones and we must be far away."

A man, his body bruised and broken, stumbled through the darkening woods. Branches snapped as he pushed his way through them. Blood trickled down his face where twigs had caught him and left their mark. He paid no attention either to the pain of his wounds or the throbbing ache in his left arm. Fear filled his mind, pushing out all thoughts of his own comfort and reflecting in his grey eyes. From time to time he glanced over his shoulder as if he was being chased. A wolf howled mournfully and the bleeding man rushed on ever faster. He fell once, but something was driving him, and he lifted himself up and pressed forward.

By Sokarjo Stormwillow

Finally, the woods ended, almost abruptly, and the man stopped short, gazing up at the sight before him. Across a rolling green field of waving grass and scattered yew trees, speckled with the purple of summer asters, a massive grey stone castle rose majestically into the dusk sky, its green and white banners flapping gently in the cool summer breeze. A deep, threatening gorge ran around the castle, barring any passage. The man took a deep breath, pushed a pesky lock of bloodied blonde hair from his face, and plunged forward towards the castle. As he approached, he could see the floor of the dry ravine was littered with sharp, jagged rocks and patches of the ground seemed to be moving in its depths. A long bridge stood nearby, the only way to cross the ravine. A small guard tower was situated near the bridge and the bridge itself was heavily patrolled and guarded.

The captain of the guard was making his daily rounds of inspection and saw the wounded man lurching towards him. He called out, beckoning to two soldiers standing close by.

"Treyvis! Mahlon! Bring me that man!"

The two armored men leapt to do his bidding as the captain called to a slender, silent guard with a patch across his left eye. "Jerril! Summon Cleric Saldor!"

The man fell to his knees just as the soldiers reached him. They caught him by the arms and pulled him up, leading him, limping, to Captain Guresh.

"What is your name?" Guresh demanded. The man gasped a few words, then fainted from loss of blood as an astonished look passed over the captain's face.

"Get him inside the walls! Now!" The men nodded and rushed past him into the great fortress, dragging the flaccid body. Guresh surveyed the surrounding tree line uneasily, then followed them through the gates.

Within moments the stranger was placed on a cot in a small hut. The dusk light stole softly in through the glassless windows and the sounds of crickets welcoming the encroaching darkness began to filter in through the open door. A man in a long robe the color of cornflowers swept in, taking his place by the man's still body.

"Saldor," the captain greeted him. "He lost consciousness just as we reached him. I believe he has an important message."

"And why is that, Captain Guresh?" the cleric answered coolly.

Guresh spoke softly into the cleric's ear.

Saldor nodded. "Then I shall see that he recovers. An assistant would be helpful."

The captain turned to the two men waiting behind him. "Mahlon, stay and lend your aid to Saldor. Treyvis, I want to know the moment this man is conscious."

"Yes, sir!" Treyvis and Mahlon chorused.

"Saldor, I go to the king. I shall return as quickly as I can."

As the captain strode swiftly from the hut, Saldor turned to Mahlon. "Bring me the skins of the emerald snakes that are just beyond the edge of the woods. I shall need two." Mahlon nodded and dashed from the hut as Saldor turned to Treyvis. "You, boy. Make yourself useful and bring me a bucket of water from the spring. Hurry now lad, your captain must not be kept waiting."

"Yes, sir," and Treyvis sped off to do as he had been bidden.

Saldor looked calmly into the pallid face before him, noting the gaunt features and the ashen skin. Quickly, but unhurriedly, he began to loosen the man's sweat-dampened shirt and pull off his muddy, torn boots.

Captain Guresh strode quickly up the great stone steps and through the large double doors. He beckoned for a guard on patrol to follow him.

"Gather a scouting party and search the surrounding woods for anything suspicious. And be sure all the men are armed." The guard nodded. Guresh stopped and placed his hand firmly on the guard's shoulder. "And for the safety of the king, send only the truest hearts and sharpest eyes."

"Right away, sir!" the guard dashed away and the captain walked purposefully toward a second set of double doors. The two soldiers guarding these doors stepped aside, revealing intricate engravings upon the heavy wooden panels. The royal family crest was centered in each door, surrounded by exquisitely detailed depictions of the great and noble deeds of the kingdom. Each time he saw these doors, Guresh's heart swelled with pride. He loved his country and his people, more even than his own life; a loyalty that had driven him to become the captain of the royal guard. Even now, though his alert mind was filled with worry, he paused for a moment to take in the elegant engravings before pushing both doors open wide and striding purposefully inside.

The king sat silent upon his throne, deep in thought. Nearby, behind a small desk, sat a young scribe garbed in rich greens, his pen ready to ink whatever his king demanded be written. Two sentinels stood silent, alert, and watchful, one on either side of the room and three servants were clearing away a half-eaten dinner. Guresh stepped forward, knelt to one knee, and placed his fist on the floor to steady himself, his other hand clenched behind his back.

The king looked up. "Yes, yes, my good captain. Please, stand and speak." The king's tone was wise and gentle, but weary.

The captain rose and addressed him. "Your majesty, we have just received within our walls a stranger; a man from Kerik by the look of him, whom you may be interested in."

"Oh? How so?"

"He is severely wounded and lost consciousness just as we reached him on the bridge. Saldor is with him now. The only words we heard him speak were, 'Long live King Tahlon'."

The king sat up with a start. "What?!?"

"Yes, your majesty, I believe that this is the news we have been waiting for."

The king sat back, thoughtfully. After a short pause, he spoke softly, "You say Saldor is with him?"

Guresh bowed sharply. "Yes, your majesty."

The king rose, determined. "Very well. Take me to him."

The two motionless guards sprang to life and were beside the king before Guresh could respond, ready and poised for action by their lord's side. With a loyal guard on either side, the king followed his trusted captain out the great doors, down the corridors, and into the courtyard. A light breeze caressed the stout oaks and whispering willows, stirring the leaves and beckoning to those who paid it any heed. Low lying bushes clustered round nearly every tree, post and pole, and brilliant marigolds and snapdragons basked in the setting sun, spreading their vivid colors between stone paths and under open windows. Across the courtyard and past a trickling fountain, a small hut sat shadowed by a great oak and two small birch trees, a simple shelter for wayfarers and traveling minstrels. As the two powerful men entered the hut, the guards remaining outside, Treyvis and Mahlon leapt to their feet to bow low. Jerril, the one-eyed guard, bowed stiffly and stepped back into the shadows of the darkening hut.

"Greetings, Kilme," Saldor spoke coolly, placing an emerald snake skin across the pale, still face on the cot before him. He did not turn nor look up, nor bow in reverence.

"Saldor," the king said, anxiously. "Has he awakened?"

Not yet," Saldor replied, closing his eyes and placing his hands atop the glistening skins. "But soon."

Every man in the room stood motionless and still, barely daring to breathe. Crickets sang softly outside, the trees whispered to one another, and a small lantern cast dancing shadows and flickers of light across the walls and the faces of the anxious men. Only Jerril stood sheathed wholly in darkness. Saldor's lips moved slowly, at first with no sound. Soon a soft whisper sifted through the room. It was a light voice, almost feminine, and filled the room with a gentle breeze, tossing the flickers from the lantern even more crazily throughout the small room. There were no words, only unintelligible whispers, yet a strange feeling swelled in each heart, leaving the waiting men bewildered, but exhilarated.

The Tale of Tyrfing

Then the whispers faded and Saldor lifted the skins from the man's face. The color had returned to the pallid countenance and within moments the man's pale blue eyes fluttered open. He looked around, slightly dazed, until his gaze rested upon Saldor's gentle face.

"Welcome back, my friend," Saldor said, softly.

"I must speak with King Kilme," the man moaned weakly.

Saldor rose and stepped back as King Kilme drew forward. "What news have you brought me, good man?" the king asked, a mixture of fear and hope sweeping across his withered face.

"I--- am Gren, my lord. I am Jaykon Jordahn's closest comrade and brother. I--- bring news from Kerik."

There was a terrible pause as the man drew a ragged breath.

"Jaykon and his wife, Traida, who is my sister, and four of their young children--- were--- murdered by Kermain, not a fortnight hence. I found no sign of his two eldest children--- a boy and a girl--- nor--- my aged mother."

With every pained word, Kilme's heart sank. Gren closed his eyes, his message delivered, and slept deeply. Kilme stepped back and looked sadly at Guresh.

"Then all is lost." He spoke slowly, his voice full of pain and hopelessness. "When my time comes, the Duke of Charike will devour West Damor, as he has done with our Eastern borders."

Guresh objected passionately. "There is still hope, my lord. We do not yet know the fate of Jaykon's missing children."

Kilme shook his graying head. "No, Captain Guresh, Kermain would not have spared them. I have failed and Tahlon's death will go unavenged. I have failed. May the Gods forgive me." His words became softer and he turned and left the hut, mourning heavily.

Saldor, his hand resting lightly on Gren's shoulder, gazed at Guresh calmly and without fear or sorrow.

Guresh hesitated, then spoke fiercely. "I refuse to abandon hope. We will not rest until the children are found." And with that, Guresh strode swiftly away as a wise smile played about the cleric's lips.

Chapter Six

Mushbahc felt a strange sensation swell through him as he carried the little girl in his arms. She felt so tender, so helpless. Her fragile body relaxed in his embrace as she slumbered peacefully. She seemed to fully trust him, regardless of his monstrous appearance.

Mushbahc had been raised with barbarians from the Northern Mountains in Srak; he had hated the continual snow and ice, but had grown accustomed to the cold. When he had grown old enough, he had learned the skills of tracking and exploring. He was not the only troll dwelling with the barbarians, for his father was also warmly welcomed into their world. He remembered his mother only a very little and the barbarians would not speak of her, nor would his father. He knew she could not have been a troll, for his appearance differed much from his father's. His ears were pointed like his father's and he had the sharp teeth, large features and frightening visage. But his eyes were softer and his skin a much lighter shade of green. His hair, thick and matted much like his father's, was also lighter and sometimes even smoother. He carried himself much the way his father did, but didn't lurch like most trolls. His legs were longer and he strode with more grace than the rest of his race. He enjoyed a mud grub now and again, or a tasty toad with supper, but for the most part his meals consisted of barbarian food: meat, bread, stew and frothy beer. He had developed a taste for the victuals, much to his barbarian grandmother's delight.

Colly stirred then slept on, and the troll was filled with an anomalous desire to protect these humans, especially the golden-haired cherub in his arms.

Perhaps that is why he did not notice the stirring in the woods nearby.

But Freeno did. The dog's ears perked up and he stopped dead in his tracks, listening and sniffing the air. Mushbahc heard a faint whine from the mutt and froze. His pointed ears listened intently and Seaghan and Gemaine dared not move, lest they distract their trollish protector. Mushbahc motioned for the boy and his grandmother to kneel in the tall grass, out of sight. He placed the sleeping girl in Gemaine's arms. Swiftly and silently, he drew closer to the hushed sounds and disappeared from their sight. Gemaine clutched her slumbering granddaughter as Seaghan struggled to keep Freeno quiet. Their hearts pounded as they sat motionless, awaiting Mushbahc's return. Colly stirred and whimpered, and Gemaine quickly clamped a withered hand over her pouting mouth. Moments later, they heard footsteps approaching. Freeno whimpered, stood up, whimpered again then bounded away into the tall grass, his cord slipping through Seaghan's fingers.

"Freeno!" Seaghan called in a hoarse whisper. "Come back!"

Gemaine grabbed Seaghan's shoulder and pulled him sharply back. He trembled beneath her bony fingers as the footsteps drew closer.

Suddenly, they heard a short, shrill bark followed by a gruff cry of surprise. Unable to bear his fear any longer, Seaghan leapt to his feet. Mushbahc stood nearby and a tall, elderly man stood next to him, wide grins spread across both faces. On the ground beside them a dwarf lay on his back with Freeno standing on his broad chest, licking his face.

"Get this blasted beast off of me!" the dwarf roared.

Later that night, the small party sat around a warm campfire, feasting on the meat of a buck that Mushbahc had bested. Millions of stars filled the night sky, and a great hickory tree stood just close enough to catch the flickering light of the campfire.

"It's mighty good, m'lady," the dwarf said as Gemaine refilled Mushbahc's plate.

"Thank you, sir," she responded. Never before had she served such an unusual company. Mushbahc was odd enough, but she had never once met a wizard or a dwarf. Halflings, elves and men she knew, but this quiet wizard and his bearded companion were like no other she had ever met. She handed Mushbahc's plate to him and smiled. Like a child, the troll eagerly accepted the plate with both hands and quickly began to clean it. Berinder smiled at him and chuckled.

"Your father always hated meat like this," the wizard said. "He would leave camp, always looking for mud grubs or some other strange creature to satisfy his hunger."

Mushbahc grinned broadly. "That's because he never ate Gemaine's food."

Gemaine smiled even more. He was the strangest troll she'd ever seen. He was great, strong and terrible; and yet, so gentle. His face was that of a monster and his race was notorious for their bloodlust and violence, yet he seemed so innocent and kind; and his smile, so broad and cheerful. But she knew he wasn't like this all the time. She had seen him the night before as he sat guarding them whilst they slept. He had been so solemn and almost--- sad. There was some pain in his past, she was certain of it. Something quite terrible that she, as curious as she may be, did not care to know.

The wizard pulled her from her thoughts. "If you would be so kind, my lady." He rose to his feet, towering above all except Mushbahc. "I must speak with you in private, if you will." The two of them strode slowly away from the camp, their steps illuminated by Berinder's staff.

Colly leapt to her feet and ran to Mushbahc. She climbed up onto his lap as she had done on the nights her father had been home, and snuggled down into the astonished troll's arms.

"I like you Mushbahc," she giggled with joy.

Mushbahc was struck speechless. Seaghan rose to his feet and strode over to them.

"Yes, Mushbahc. We could never have gotten this far without you." He extended his young hand. Mushbahc looked deep into the boy's eyes. The events of the past fortnight had changed Seaghan from a child into a young man. Mushbahc saw a great strength and a steel will in the boy, and knew in his heart that this lad would grow up to be a great man and a king of men. The troll stretched out a large, rough and dirty hand and grasped Seaghan's small one. That night a bond was formed between the two that promised never to be shaken.

The next morning, the sun winked down at them, stroking their faces with its warm strands and calling them to rise. It had just peeked over the top of the trees, but was rising steadily. Yellow spikes of goldenrod hung round about them, scattered near copses of hickory, oak, and a solitary sprawling cottonwood. Sprinklings of lacy wild carrot, pale daisies, and sunset-orange milkweed added brilliant color to the green and brown grasses of the land; tall brome, goose grass, foxtail and barley. Mushbahc, already awake and prepared to travel, touched Gemaine's shoulder gently. As she looked up at him sleepily, his deep voice roused her.

"Gemaine should wake the young ones now. We leave soon."

The old woman nodded sleepily and struggled to her feet. Mushbahc placed a steady hand on her arm and helped her to rise. She nodded her thanks and approached the sleeping children. Berinder, also already awake, was attempting to stir the slumbering dwarf. His snores shook deep in his belly and Berinder seemed to have little effect on him. Finally, the wizard stood and began jabbing his staff into the dwarf's side. At long last, the dwarf awoke, muttering and growling. He swept his hands across the ground, searching for something. When he looked over at the children, he sighed and lay back on the ground.

"This twill be a long journey," he muttered. Berinder smiled and glanced over at Colly, snuggled serenely into Kundin's blanket.

Gemaine gently woke first Seaghan, then Colly and bade them rise. Colly rubbed her eyes and yawned. Then she pulled herself to her feet, rolled the blanket rather clumsily up in her small arms and strode towards the dwarf.

"Thank you for giving me your blanket, Mr. Kundin," she said sweetly, handing him the grass-covered cloth. The dwarf beamed at her as she turned back towards her grandmother. He looked sideways at the wizard and shrugged, gruffly clearing his throat.

After they had eaten, Berinder spoke softly to Mushbahc as the others gathered their belongings and prepared to set out.

"Travel quickly and take care of that boy."

Mushbahc nodded. "Do not trouble yourself. He will be safe with me."

"I know he will. You have a good heart, Mushbahc. But be very careful as you enter Damor. Men will not be likely to trust a troll, even a half-troll. Farewell, my friend."

After many tearful embraces, the small party divided. Mushbahc and Seaghan set out in a northwesterly direction for Damor and the castle in Cherin. Kundin, Berinder, Gemaine and Colly set their course mostly west, headed for the shores of Tobli and the ship that would carry them to the Isle of Élas, the home of the elves. It was a painful parting, but the spirits of all were full of hope.

Mushbahc stirred restlessly. Seaghan slumbered lightly nearby, but the troll sensed an uneasy air about the woods and he could not sleep. He had been aware of it since Berinder had left. He felt as if perhaps they were being followed. His gaze swept slowly over the dark tree-line, the oak, elm and sycamore forest standing tall and shadowy against the night sky.

But as hard as he tried to stay alert, he was tired and his body drooped, gradually giving way to sleep. And as he slept, he dreamt.

Mushbahc sat up, terrified and dripping with sweat. He looked around to regain his senses and sighed softly, brushing his brow with the back of his hand. He could recall very little of his dream, yet the images of flesh melting away from bone flashed through his mind, illuminated by a green mist and accented by tortured screams. He remembered mostly fear and death. His body slowly stopped trembling as he closed his eyes and willed his racing heart to calm itself.

Suddenly he heard a twig snap. Seaghan, who had not slept very heavily since the night they began this journey, was awake in an instant. Mushbahc motioned for him to be quiet and the boy nodded. The two of them rose slowly from the ground and stood still, listening.

The Tale of Tyrfing

The fire had long since sputtered out, but the moon was full and bright and the sky was full of stars. The trees around them were tall and the underbrush was quite dense, making it difficult for the troll to move about quietly. They were on the borders of Kerik and Damor, on the fringe of a shadowy wood. Mushbahc knew that it was common for raiders and thieves to lie in waiting in a forest, and he would take no chances. He crept as slowly, as silently as he could into the brush. Seaghan followed, terrified at the thought of staying behind alone.

What they saw that night haunted them for years to come. As they hid in the brush and peered into the darkness, their hearts raced and even the mighty troll trembled. He had never seen anything like these images before in his long trollish life.

She was beautiful. Her long white hair fell in wispy waves around her face, billowing gently in the occasional breeze. A soft white gown was draped gracefully over her lovely frame and her grey-toned feet were bare. Seaghan's eyes were drawn to the intricate and beautiful designs on her skin. They appeared to be some sort of tribal markings, a decoration not uncommon to dark elves. Mushbahc's eyes, however, focused on the elf's remarkable face. She was the most stunning drow he had ever seen. The shadow elves he had met in Berea were certainly lovely, but they were simple when compared to this drow's flawless beauty. However, it was not her breathtaking visage that held the troll's gaze, but her eyes. They were gazing straight ahead, unblinking. The lack of pupils or irises gave the lady's eyes a ghastly white solidity. She walked as if in a trance, not appearing to hear or see anything around her.

But although her eyes were certainly frightening, Mushbahc was not prepared for the vision that followed her.

He was dead; as dead as ghouls can be. He had once been a drow, of that Mushbahc was sure. But now he was a mixture of undead elf, phantom and skeleton. His entire form was transparent and ghostly. Part of his face was simply blanched skull, while the rest consisted of decaying flesh hanging laxly from bone. His hands were of the same appearance and the rest of his frame covered in a tattered cloak. There was no color in him; not in his rotting flesh nor in his hooded cloak. He had no legs, the lower half of his body becoming nothing more than a ghostly mass, the torn cloak hanging loosely. The apparition's cloak did not blow in the wind, nor did his thin wispy hair, of which there was little left. It was as if he was merely floating through the atmosphere and not a part of it at all. A cold chill ran down Mushbahc's spine, and Seaghan began to tremble. Mushbahc took hold of his scale-like cloak and draped it over the boy's body, hiding his eyes from the scene and his presence from the terrifying pair.

By Sokarjo Stormwillow

The phantom's eyes glowed red and the girl stopped less than a stone's throw from Mushbahc. He could hear her haunting voice as she spoke softly to the ghoul.

"Master," her voice was quiet, but sounded unearthly and hollow.

The ghoul's voice seemed to echo as if he were deep inside a cave. "I sense something... familiar." Mushbahc barely breathed and his fingers touched his sword's hilt. "But I care not enough to interrupt my journey. Onward!"

"Yes, Master," the girl replied. She seemed to be held captive by some unnatural power.

As they swept away into the shadows, Mushbahc noticed something. The phantom's essence seemed to be streaming from a piece of metal on the girl's ankle. It was a black band bearing some sort of intricate design. It somehow seemed familiar to Mushbahc and he felt as if he had seen the symbols somewhere before. He also noticed something else that he found quite perplexing and haunting. Dangling like a trophy from the skeletal arm of the undead phantom was a long black ponytail.

Chapter Seven

Gemaine could not believe her eyes. She stood on a grassy cliff beside Berinder, gazing in awe at the rocky shores and the crystal sea before her. Billows of snowy white sails slid gracefully along the glowing horizon and she could hear the cries of seagulls dance across the sparkling waters. The setting sun caught the ocean waves in its golden light and it seemed to Gemaine as if the ocean was sprinkled with shimmering diamonds.

Berinder smiled at her. "My dear," he said softly. "This is the Theilas Ocean."

"It's so--- lovely!" Gemaine gasped. "I--- I have never seen anything like it!"

At that moment, Kundin and Colly came up behind them, Freeno at their heels. Colly gasped. "Grandmamma! Look at all that water! Oh! Will we have to swim?" whereupon the child began to whimper softly.

"Now, now, child," said Berinder, kneeling beside her. "Why the tears?"

"Oh, Mr. Berinder, sir," she sobbed. "I cannot swim. I shall surely drown!" And she tossed her small arms around his long neck, nearly toppling him over and began sobbing onto his shoulder.

Berinder smiled and patted her back gently. "Come my child," he said. Colly rubbed her hands across her face, attempting to wipe away her tears. "We will not have to swim," the wizard comforted her. "Follow me. I shall show you how we will move across the ocean." At this, the elderly wizard rose and took the girl by the hand. Kundin tugged the red cord round Freeno's neck and they turned to follow the others.

The group moved carefully down the grassy slope to their right and soon their eyes were greeted by a most welcome sight. Spread across the shore before them was nestled a small seacoast village. Colly stared in wonder at the strange, new sight that greeted her astonished gaze. The little bustling town was alive with new sounds and colors. There were vendors selling all sorts of wonderful things; from fruits and vegetables, to pottery and furs, to jewelry and fine silks. There were cattle bellowing, sheep bleating and dogs barking. Colly saw wild boars in cages, dancers twirling in the streets and horses drawing wagons filled with colorful wares. She heard music from a small group of men on the corner near the dancers, and she heard bells ringing in the tower of a large building on the edge of town. Children ran passed her laughing and cheering, and she would have joined them had Berinder not a firm grip on her hand. Most of the people in the village were human, like her, but she saw others as well; a few colossal men, cheerful halflings and elves mostly. A dwarf was stepping out of a nearby tavern and Kundin strode towards him. The two stood conversing for several moments, then bowed low to each other and parted. Kundin rejoined them and addressed Berinder.

"Berinder, sir, I have obtained safe lodgings for us all."

"Very good, Kundin. Take Gemaine and Colly and I will find you as soon as I have bartered our passage on the morrow's ship."

"Aye, sir," answered Kundin, with a nod of his head. "We shall be in the Onyx Inn, just yonder."

"Very well." Berinder turned to Gemaine. "My dear, rest in peace. No one will harm you or your granddaughter here. I shall return swiftly." And with that, the wizard was lost in the crowd.

"Follow me," boomed Kundin's gruff voice.

Gemaine took Colly's hand and followed the dwarf toward the inn, Kundin leading the dog. When they stepped inside the large musty room, they were greeted by the pleasing aroma of hearty stew and freshly baked bread. Kundin led them to a table against the far wall and motioned for a barmaid. A very rotund woman with bright rosy cheeks and curly red hair approached them, wiping her damp, ample hands on her once-white apron and beaming at the little girl with cheery eyes, the color of strong tea.

"We'll be needin' food. There are those of us here, and one more to join us soon." Kundin told her, tying Freeno's cord to his wrist.

"Aye, of course!" the woman exclaimed, clapping her hands together in delight. "An' would 'e like some milk for the bairn?" she asked, glancing up at Gemaine.

Gemaine nodded shyly and the woman hurried away. Colly climbed up in a chair and looked around wide-eyed, her feet dangling above the floor, kicking in a restless fashion. Gemaine, too, was silent as she glanced around the room. Nearly every table was filled with strange patrons from distant lands. A few seemed to be locals, workmen and craftsmen making their living off the travelers who passed through their coastal town. But

The Tale of Tyrfing

most were obviously from other, far-off places. Kundin was standing at a nearby table, conversing with the dwarf from before, a red-haired burly man who smiled cheerfully and laughed heartily, as well as two others-- a black-haired silent dwarf with far-seeing eyes, and a wise, grey-haired dwarf who seemed to be older even than the dwarven lord. A few tables were occupied by grisly looking characters, unshaven and unkempt, rowdy and loud. In one corner sat an odd looking pair-- one was an elf, dressed in brown, but Gemaine could see little of his face or form, which was shrouded in a dark green cloak. His companion was similar to a human in appearance, but a giant of a man, standing nine feet tall or more, with very broad shoulders and toned muscles. He too wore a green cloak, though it was thrown back on his shoulders, revealing a sunny face and bright eyes, framed by a tangled mass of golden waves. A barbarian sword swung from his hip, but he also carried a longbow, crafted by the wood elves, slung across his back, along with a quiver full of arrows. The elf was solemn and spoke in soft whispers but his hefty comrade smiled and laughed and occasionally slapped the table while throwing his head back, clearly absorbed in his own amusement. Other tables held various assortments of men, halflings, dwarves, and elves, but Gemaine's gaze was always drawn again by the pair in the back.

"Gemaine?" Kundin's deep voice brought the old lady sharply out of her deep thoughts. She looked around wildly, trying to establish her whereabouts. She had dozed off and now the dim tavern was nearly empty. Colly too was sleeping, curled up like a small kitten in her chair. Kundin was standing beside Gemaine, along with the three other dwarves and Berinder, Freeno sitting patiently by. There were no others in the large room except the innkeeper and one of the maids.

"Come, lassie," said the red-headed dwarf. "I'll show 'e to your room."

"Thank you," Gemaine responded, in a voice still weary from their travels. She arose and took a weary step forward, then turned back to Colly. The ebony-haired dwarf motioned her on. "I'll bring her," he assured her. He lifted the small child up into his arms and carried her gently up the stairs. Gemaine ascended slowly, one trembling hand on the staircase and one on the shoulder of the red-headed dwarf.

"Me name be Olak, lassie," he grinned at her. "Olak Amberstone. An' ye may lean on me as much as 'e likes. I be a stout and hardy fool."

Gemaine chuckled softly. The elderly dwarf led them up the sturdy staircase, down a dimly lit hall, to a door that was standing open. "Inside here, lads," he instructed the other dwarves. "Madam, there be a bed all made up an' ready fer ya over against the wall there," he said, pointing. The somber, gray-haired dwarf entered the room carrying a tray with two cups upon it, brimming with milk.

"Ah," said Olak. "An' here be Ulrin with yer evenin' glass. Drink up, lassie. It be warm and'll help 'e sleep."

"Thank you," Gemaine nodded as she took one of the cups and sipped from it. It was indeed warm and spiced, and Gemaine closed her eyes as she savored its delicious goodness.

"Goodnight, Gemaine," Berinder said, his gentle voice soothing to her spirit. "I will come and wake you in the morning. Sleep well until then."

During the quiet night, a drowsy Gemaine thought she heard low voices and pained sobbing from the room next to theirs. Though at first she was sleepily anxious for the clearly despairing soul, she wearily determined it was none of her business what others spoke of, and promptly forgot all about it as she drifted off to a deeper sleep.

The next morning, Berinder roused Gemaine and bade her come to breakfast. "Our ship hauls anchor in a short time," he told her. "Best come eat and we will find some clothing for Colly before we leave."

A meal of porridge and fresh bread awaited them in the tavern and they ate their fill. The plump waitress from the night before handed them a large basket with instructions not to open it until lunchtime. Gemaine thanked her profusely as Kundin lifted the basket onto his back. He groaned slightly then looked around to be sure no one had heard him. Olak had though, and immediately sprang to his side, insisting to carry the load at least as far as the ship's side. Kundin agreed only after Olak insisted his only desire was to see the lasses off and needed a proper excuse. Ulrin, the aging dwarf, and Malvid, the dark one, followed as well.

At last Gemaine and Colly were arrayed in new attire, more proper for a visit to the elfish Isle of Élas. The little girl looked like a cherub in her white dress, which billowed like fluffy clouds around her petite frame. Her grandmother looked just as lovely, though more regal and wise in a soft gown of rich browns and deepest reds. They were swept aboard the waiting ship. Gemaine watched as the land shrank then vanished into the distance. She thought sadly of her grandson and how much he had endured thus far, and had yet to endure if he even made it as far as Damor. She sighed and looked around at the various people on the ship's decks.

Suddenly, she noticed a familiar figure. It was the elf from the tavern. She was certain of it, even if she still could not see his face. *I wonder what he can be going to Élas for?* She thought, watching him curiously. *And where is the other?*

The Tale of Tyrfing

Chapter Eight

Mushbahc was wading through the tall field grasses of southern Damor beneath a glaring sun, when he heard the cries of an animal in pain. He turned quickly to follow the small screeches and Seaghan followed him silently, too deep in his own disturbed thoughts to wonder what the troll was doing. They soon arrived in a clearing; a small meadow, dotted with motley colored wildflowers and framed on three sides by close cropped oaks and maples. A small brook wiggled its way through the far side of the clearing and beyond it rippled lush green hills, seemingly untouched by the cruel heat of the summer sun. Seaghan, roused suddenly from his contemplations, pointed excitedly to the brook's muddy bank where a tiny ball of fur thrashed wildly about beneath the dappled shade of an ancient alder.

"Look, Mushbahc!" he cried softly. "That little creature is caught in a trap!"

Mushbahc sprinted forward, slowing his pace as he drew nearer. He began speaking softly in a beautiful language Seaghan had never heard. The creature stopped writhing and watched him cautiously with its black beady eyes. It appeared to be some sort of minx, though like no other creature Seaghan had ever seen before. Its tail was long and bushy, and its body was mongoose shaped. Its snowy white fur was matted and dirty from the mud the trap was in. It had been thrashing about wildly, but now held very still, watching Mushbahc's every move. The troll continued speaking to it in the strange language and soon its pointed black nose began sniffing the air. Suddenly it let out a cry so woeful and pitiful that it was as if the very air was moaning. Seaghan jumped slightly, startled by this sudden outcry, but Mushbahc merely chuckled. He approached the animal with less caution and immediately began to free it. When the creature was released, it ran dizzying circles around Mushbahc's legs, ran to the nearby brook and dove in. It came out perfectly clean and shook itself like a small dog, then began to lick itself to dry. Mushbahc was watching it with a giant grin on his face. Seaghan crept closer. The furry creature leapt up, ran forward and shimmied up Mushbahc's tall form to his shoulders. It perched itself there and squealed happily. Seaghan laughed and Mushbahc turned toward him.

"Lad, this is a furkle. Ever seen one of these before?" he asked the boy.

"No sir," Seaghan responded, staring in wonder and moving closer.

The furkle growled low, but Mushbahc touched its nose. The furkle silenced and looked at his rescuer, then watched Seaghan cautiously approach. When he was close enough, Mushbahc put out his huge green hand and touched Seaghan's shoulder. The furkle squealed with delight, shot down Mushbahc's arm and onto Seaghan's neck. He dashed in circles around the boy's shoulders, squealing all the while. Seaghan giggled then began laughing.

"It tickles!" he cried. Mushbahc burst into laughter. The furkle suddenly leapt into the air, soaring to Mushbahc's broad shoulder. It sat up on its haunches and began making delighted sounds, almost comparable to singing. Seaghan watched it with sparkling eyes, and in a few moments, the furkle suddenly stopped its joyful singing and leaped once more to Seaghan's shoulder.

As the boy giggled and stroked the now purring furkle, Mushbahc turned to inspect the trap. His face lost its twinkle and immediately became solemn as he lifted the offending thing out of the brook's mire.

"What is it, Mushbahc? What's wrong?" Seaghan asked, suddenly aware of his friend's shifted mood.

"Poacher's," the troll responded grimly. As if summoned by this comment, a cautious voice called out from behind them.

"Hello there, sir! Might I ask what you're about?"

Seaghan spun around to see a tall man, dressed in peasantry and watching them with shifty eyes and a nervous air. Upon seeing him, Seaghan thought instantly of a sly fox or a sneaky weasel, and was immediately distrustful of the man.

"Where'd you get that, boy? That there is a rare furkle," the man said, as if imparting great wisdom.

"He was caught in your trap," Mushbahc said, his voice deep and threatening, accented with a growl. As he said this, he turned full around, glaring angrily at the poacher and holding up the trap like a sinister trophy. His eyes flashed with hatred and his lips set in a hard line about his protruding teeth.

The man hesitated not once, fled terrified into the woods and, the reader must know, was not seen within a five hundred mile radius ever again.

Mushbahc destroyed the trap in his bare hands, then turned to Seaghan. The troll brightened and smiled widely at Seaghan. The furkle seemed satisfied as well, and leapt once more onto the troll's towering shoulders.

The Tale of Tyrfing

"Come on, lad," sad Mushbahc with a wink "We should be going."

"You mean you're going to keep it?" Seaghan asked, excitedly.

"Aye, lad," Mushbahc nodded. "I haven't a choice. When you rescue a furkle, you're stuck with it for life. They are very loyal fellows and very protective."

"He seems so harmless," Seaghan objected.

"Aye, but in that you'd be mistaken. Furkles may seem cute enough, but in truth they are quite ferocious. Especially this one here." Mushbahc nodded towards the smiling furkle.

"But why this one?"

"Because, lad. This one is a rare white furkle. They're mighty fine warriors and excellent trackers. And there's only one born to a family of furkles every one hundred years." Mushbahc added with a grin. "Think I'm going to name him Dragyn."

Seaghan was tired and his muscles ached. They had been walking for weeks, sleeping on the hard ground. But though he was weary, he had enjoyed his travel with Mushbahc. The troll had taught him much about tracking, building campfires, hunting, and surviving in the wilderness. These were lessons he would gladly learn and remember, and someday could save his life. Seaghan had traveled many times with his father, mother, and grandmother, usually running for their lives. Now he feared nothing. He had a troll to protect him and even without that presence, Seaghan was learning to face his fears.

Suddenly Mushbahc stopped and Seaghan behind him. "What is it?" he asked.

"We're here."

Seaghan pushed through the branches to stand beside Mushbahc. Before them rose a majestic stone castle, its green and white banners flapping in the afternoon breeze. Seaghan looked down into the deep gorge that ran around the castle and saw the floor to be littered with sharp, jagged rocks and very little water. It seemed to him as if patches of the ground were moving.

"What's down there?" he asked.

"Snakes," the troll replied. "Deadly snakes."

Seaghan stepped back from the edge of the gorge, nervously. "How do we get across?" he asked, looking up at Mushbahc.

The troll's answer was slightly muffled for he had just covered his entire face, but for his eyes, with his cloak. His arms and legs were also covered, leaving no green skin to show.

"The bridge."

Seaghan's gaze swept slowly to his right, his eyes finally resting on the bridge. It was a long, garrisoned drawbridge, made of sturdy stone and accented with iron and steel. A small stone tower stood near it and held two almost unmoving guards. Several soldiers paced the bridge, their bright steel amour glinting in the afternoon sun, the edges of the plated metal trimmed in rich greens and silver.

As they drew near, two of the guards saw them and rushed forward. "Halt!" cried one. "Who are you and what is your business in Cherin?"

Seaghan and Mushbahc stopped. "I am Seaghan," said the boy, his voice bearing a nervous twinge. "Son of Jaykon Jordahn."

"Treyvis!" gasped the second soldier. "It's him! The one Captain Guresh intends to find!"

"Mahlon! Fetch the Captain!" Treyvis turned toward Seaghan and knelt to one knee. "I know you're the one," he murmured respectfully. "You look just like those paintings in the great halls. The ones of High King Tahlon."

Seaghan bowed his head to the kneeling soldier then looked up past him. All the other guards on the bridge were kneeling as well save for the three approaching him. One was the young Mahlon, and with him came two others. The one in the center must be the Captain, Seaghan thought, still nervous. The tall man strode with purpose and a touch of excitement. He wore amour much like the rest, but pinned to his broad shoulders was a rich green cape. The man beside him was thin and spindly, his grey hair thinning badly, and he wore a patch across his left eye. As soon as they stood before him, they all dropped to one knee beside Treyvis.

"Your lordship," Guresh said, in a strong, clear voice as he arose. "Please come with me. His Majesty, King Kilme is waiting for you." He turned to Mushbahc. "You are welcome stranger, if you are he to whom we are indebted for this boy's life and presence." The Captain extended his hand to express his gratitude. "Come, man. Do not fear my hand," Guresh said with a warm smile.

Mushbahc shrugged and extended his hand as well. The men gasped as the folds of his cloak fell back to reveal a giant green hand, with nails black and sharp.

Guresh drew his sword. "Boy, come away from there. This is no man, but a troll!"

Seaghan leapt in front of Mushbahc and held up his hands, quickly losing all sense of uncertainty. "Put away your sword, Captain!" he demanded. After a short moment's hesitation, he added fiercely, "If you indeed believe me to be your future king, then you will put away your sword immediately!" Guresh hesitated a second more, then tentatively sheathed his sword. Mushbahc proudly rested his huge hands on Seaghan's shoulders. Seaghan's voice was loud and strong as he spoke again. "This is my rescuer and my guide to this land and city. He is indeed part troll but he is a good man. Therefore I wish... demand for you to send word to all who dwell within these walls not to fear him, but to respect him. He is not to be harmed in any way. If any man so much as raises a hand to him, he will lose that hand."

The Tale of Tyrfing

Guresh nodded. "Aye, your lordship. You are young, but you have the command of a true king. Mahlon! Treyvis! Send word to all who are in the city that they are not to raise arms against the troll." As the two obeyed and dashed away, Guresh turned back to Mushbahc. "I beg your forgiveness, sir. I have offended you and the heir to the throne. Please allow me to shake your hand, distrusting man to good man."

Mushbahc nodded. "Your desire is to protect the boy. As is mine." And he once again extended his green hand. Guresh gripped it firmly.

Captain Guresh led them through the enormous gates and into the city. They walked along the cobblestone path, past well-built houses and busy shops. The people they passed stopped to stare, as the image of their former king strode past them, head up. One by one, each of the villagers bowed low to the young man. They were so taken with the sight of their late king incarnate they hardly noticed the giant man striding behind him, still heavily cloaked.

Outside the throne room doors, Guresh motioned for them to remain, while he entered to announce them. As the doors closed behind him, Seaghan stepped up and slowly ran his hands along the engravings.

"These doors hold many stories," Mushbahc said softly, reverently.

"And I will learn them all," the boy murmured in awe.

Seaghan stepped back quickly when he heard Guresh's footsteps approaching. One door swung open and the Captain bade them enter. The door closed firmly behind them.

Inside they found an enormous room, decorated with green and white banners. A throne stood high in the back of it, with a table and chair for the scribe next to it. A long, dark green carpet lined with white silk led up to the throne and upon it slumped an elderly man. His grey hair lay listlessly upon tired shoulders and his carriage was frail. Standing before him with an air of grandeur, was a man of average height and build, dressed in gold and blue with a hat full of plumes upon his black locks. He was speaking to the king in a manner most disrespectful, dripping with the honey of deceit.

"Furthermore, your majesty," this was said with a considerable amount of scorn. "I believe that the peoples of West Damor are in need of a new leader...."

"Yes," agreed the king heartily, standing up and striding towards Seaghan. His face had lost its dejected look and adopted one of pure joy as he approached the boy. "And that new ruler is here at last." With these last words, Kilme had reached Seaghan and knelt before him, tears streaming down his aged cheeks. Seaghan watched him solemnly, a lump in his throat, as he remembered his grandmother's tale, and was filled with a great admiration for this weary king before him.

The man who was speaking looked at Seaghan with anger and disbelief, then turned his attentions to Kilme and smiled an evil grin. "Look," said he to his guard. "Look at what a weak and spineless man rules our western lands." The guard did not respond nor move nor was there any change in his emotionless expression, but that did not seem to matter to his lord. "One who cries in the presence of babes and cannot even keep his people together."

Seaghan had heard quite enough. He stepped past Kilme and demanded, "And who are you, sir, to belittle a man so great as this?" His voice was young, telling of his fourteen years, but it was strong and clear and revealed also his inherited authority.

The man laughed a wicked laugh, his hazel eyes filled with bitterness and malice. "Child, I am Zaris, Duke of Charike, and ruler of East Damor."

"You are ruler of nothing," Seaghan retorted. "For I intend to unite Damor once again. Your reign is over, Duke."

"Impudent boy! You have no power over me!" the Duke screamed, his face turning a bright shade of red.

"He does!" returned Kilme passionately, taking his stand beside Seaghan. "He has power over both you and me! He is Seaghan, grandson of Tahlon and ruler of all Damor!"

Zaris' eyes widened in disbelief and anger. "It cannot be! It is impossible! He is an impostor!" The Duke's hands had begun to tremble. Suddenly maddened, he snatched up the ornate golden dagger at his hip and rushed at Seaghan. Seaghan took a step back, though no fear showed in his face.

In an instant, Mushbahc tossed back his cloak and lunged at the raging Duke. He caught the man by both arms and held him tight. Zaris' screams of rage and anger turned to pitiful screeches of terror. The guard leapt forward, but his path was immediately cut off by Guresh's sword.

"Captain Guresh," said Seaghan in a calm voice.

"Yes, your majesty?"

"Have both these men locked up on charges of treason and attempted murder."

"Yes, your majesty," Guresh grinned and bowed.

Two soldiers began to drag the guard from the room and two more took hold of Zaris. Mushbahc glared at him and, baring his teeth, he growled low and mean. The furkle upon his shoulder did likewise and Zaris whimpered then fainted in the arms of his captors. Mushbahc turned back to Seaghan, a wide, mischievous grin on his face. Seaghan smiled broadly.

Kilme turned to Seaghan and clapped him on the back. "Splendid," he exclaimed. "You were remarkable, my boy. You shall make this kingdom great once again. I can feel it in my bones."

Chapter Nine

The travelers had been informed by the ship's captain that they would be landing the following day. The crew bustled about the deck, anxious to put aboard on dry land and take a brief reprieve from the perilous sea. Gemaine sat on the deck in a rocking chair that the crew had eagerly provided. They said she reminded them of their mothers and they were happy to do just about anything to ensure her comfort on the voyage to Élas. She sat now, rocking and listening to the gulls cry and the waves splash against the strong sides of the ship, knitting and watching Kundin and Colly play. That is, if you can call it playing when it involves a dwarven lord. Kundin was attempting to teach the young girl to play chess, but was having little luck, and Gemaine chuckled softly at his rough attempts.

Berinder was off somewhere having "intellectual conversations" as he liked to call them. Gemaine knew that it was far more possible that he was smoking his long-stem pipe or drinking a mug of ale than anything. She knew what weaknesses wizards had, but she was not about to condemn him for either.

Colly was giggling and squealing now and Gemaine looked up from her needlework. The young girl had taken Kundin's wooden king piece and was running in circles round the deck with the dwarf in hot pursuit. He was calling out for her to bring the piece back, chuckling under his beard all the while. Suddenly, a door swung open and Colly ran right into the man exiting onto the deck. Kundin followed, unable to stop, and the three of them tumbled to the deck. Gemaine rose quickly from her seat and rushed over to see that all were unharmed, then stopped in sudden surprise as she recognized the barbarian from the tavern.

He immediately began apologizing and pulled the elderly dwarf to his feet. "Forgive me, sir, I meant no harm." When Kundin was upright, the giant man lifted Colly up. "Are ya alright, lassie?" he asked.

"Yes, sir," she replied then stared at his bulky body and blonde locks. "What did you eat that made you grow so big?" she asked innocently.

The big man began to laugh a thunderous roar. "Well, lass, I ate my vegetables," here he knelt down in front of her. "Do you like vegetables?"

Colly put her hands on her cheeks and made a face. She shook her head and ran away. The barbarian resumed his roaring guffaw and Kundin joined him with his own laughter. Gemaine chuckled and returned to her chair and neglected needle. Kundin turned cheerfully to the barbarian.

"An' what be your name? I don't think I've seen ya on this boat before."

"Aye, my friend won't let me come out, 'cause he says I'm too loud and draw too much attention," replied the barbarian with a gutsy laugh. "My name is Galayvin, friend," and he extended his hand to the dwarf.

"And I am Kundin, of the Kaladure Clan in Gamlin," replied the dwarf as he shook the barbarian's hand firmly.

"Aye? I too am from Gamlin, though I tend to dwell above ground most days."

"Is that so? Then it is an honor, friend."

At that moment, Berinder came round the corner, puffing on his pipe.

"Berinder, we have a new friend in our midst. This be Galayvin, from the woods of Gamlin."

Berinder looked at him curiously. "Oh?"

"Aye, sir. At your service," Wherewith Galayvin bowed low and grinned broadly at the wizard.

"And what is your purpose aboard this ship, Galayvin?" Berinder asked.

For the first time since she had laid eyes upon the barbarian, Gemaine saw no hint of light in the barbarian's steely grey eyes, nor a smile upon his rugged face. Solemnly he spoke to Berinder.

"My friend and I come from Gamlin to Élas for word with Almyn Ostara." His voice hushed. "An evil has come to our land which must be destroyed, before it destroys those of us who remain."

"What?!?" gasped the dwarf. "What has happened in Gamlin?"

Berinder sat down upon a nearby bundle and puffed his pipe. "I think you'd best speak more of this, lad."

But before Galayvin could begin, they all heard a voice call out from the bow of the ship. "Galayvin! What did I tell you about...?" The voice did not finish, but trailed off when he saw the group assembled around his friend.

Galayvin grinned broadly once again. "Scarlyn! I want to introduce you to my new friends. This is Kundin..."

"Your majesty," the elf nodded in acknowledgment.

"Majesty?" Galayvin asked, surprised.

"Yes. Do you not remember father's tales of Kundin, Lord of the Kaladure Clan in Mount Roguk?"

"Aye that I do!" Galayvin exclaimed, excited by this new revelation. "Ya didn't tell me you were that Kundin!"

Lord Kundin merely grinned.

"Well," Galayvin continued. "This is..."

"Ah, Berinder. Greetings, noble wizard." Scarlyn said with a bow. Berinder smiled and nodded to the elf.

"Well blasted bats! Ya know all of em!" Galayvin exclaimed, exasperated.

"No," said Scarlyn calmly. "I have not yet met this lovely lady." And with that he turned to Gemaine and took her hand. "Tell me, dear maid, what is your name?"

Gemaine blushed like a young schoolgirl. "Why... I am Gemaine Brennan."

"Pleased to make your acquaintance, milady," Scarlyn said as he bowed to her. The elf was smiling sweetly, but Gemaine could not help but notice the great pain and almost ancient sadness in his mysterious hazel eyes.

That night, Scarlyn and Galayvin joined them for dinner. After dinner had been eaten, and Kundin had put Colly to bed, the men sat round the fire. Gemaine drifted off to their deep, pleasant voices. Could she have heard their words, she would probably not have slept so well, but she heard nothing and instead slept beautifully, dreaming of her younger days.

The men were gathered round a circular table, smoking pipes and drinking mead. Scarlyn began to describe to Berinder and Kundin the evil of which Galayvin had spoken.

"We know not from where this phantom comes, but he is intent on destroying the races of light." he told them.

"Have you seen the phantom?" Berinder asked.

"I have," Scarlyn nodded. "Twice I have seen him now. I have also seen his captive."

"Captive?"

"Aye," said Galayvin sadly. "Her name is Morrana. She is a dark elf, rogue, and grave robber. She is more lovely than the beams which fall from the moonlit sky... and she is possessed." Galayvin's expression again took on that demeanor of sadness and solemnity as his voice faded away.

Kundin leaned close to Scarlyn. "How does he know a drow?"

Scarlyn spoke softly back, "They met on a voyage to Berea some years ago. Her father is ambassador for the drow there."

Berinder heard. "Baral?"

"Yes, her father is Baral Tvildar. And her sister, the fair Nehru." Scarlyn nodded.

"It was said that she had vanished; killed in one of her tomb raids." Berinder wondered.

At this Galayvin looked angry. "Nothin' could kill her! Nothin' in no grave could kill Morrana!" Scarlyn hushed him and patted his giant hand as he would a puppy.

"We are traveling to see Almyn in the hopes that he will know of a way to destroy this evil phantom," Scarlyn continued. "Our elders wish to kill Morrana and in so doing they hope to destroy the Phantom. But we begged them to allow us to find another way, if one was to be found. It seems love is blind to race." This last he said softly so all but Galayvin heard.

The group fell silent and one by one they soon drifted off to sleep.

Seaghan looked fearfully at Kilme. "If you please, sir, I know nothing about the ruling of a kingdom." They stood in the throne room and had been discussing the coronation. Kilme wanted it to take place immediately.

"Never fear, lad. I shall teach you all I know. After all, I was King Tahlon's advisor, may he rest in peace, and I taught your father as well. You have the bearing of a king already." Kilme was all smiles.

Seaghan looked down at the floor. "Sir... my father... is dead."

"Aye lad, I know." Kilme replied, sadly.

"But... how?" Seaghan looked up, bewildered.

Suddenly remembering, Kilme motioned to the boy and turned to the doors, the guards at his heels. "Follow me. There's someone here whom I am sure you would want to meet."

Seaghan followed him in confused silence, Mushbahc and Dragyn not far behind. They walked down a hall lined with narrow windows, which cast slender blocks of light against the cool stone walls. They arrived at a simple oaken door and Kilme rapped on the smooth wood. Inside, they heard footsteps approaching slowly. A man dressed in deep blue robes calmly opened the door.

"Good eve, Saldor. How fares your patient?" Kilme asked.

"My lord," called a voice from within. "I can hear you smile. Please tell me you have good news. Or at least that you'll tell this confounded cleric I am well enough to leave the room!"

"I know that voice!" cried Seaghan and he pushed past the two men and into the room. "Uncle Gren!"

"Seaghan!" Gren was out of the bed in an instant. "You're alive! Odin be praised!"

"Gren, I thought he had killed you too!"

The Tale of Tyrfing

"Ha!" bragged Gren. "Never in a million years! He'd have to catch me first!"

Seaghan laughed.

"My mother? And your sister? Are they alright?" Gren asked, anxiously.

"Yes. Grandmother and Colly went with a wizard to Élas."

"Élas, eh? Good. They'll be safe there, I hope. And you came here? Not on your own, I trust." The two were speaking excitedly like children, and Saldor and Kilme could not help but smile.

"No, I had help. I could never have made it without Mushbahc."

"Mushbahc? Strange name for a man. Nonetheless, I wish to see him. Where is he?" Gren looked past the men in the doorway, searching the hall beyond.

"He is not a man."

Gren was confused. "Not a man? A dog?"

Seaghan laughed. "No... a troll."

"What? A troll? You cannot be serious?!?!"

"I am. He is actually only half troll. I want you to meet him. Mushbahc?" Seaghan called.

A giant figure came around the corner.

"Mushbahc, this is my uncle, Gren. Gren, this is Mushbahc." Seaghan watched them both carefully.

Gren needed not a second thought. He strode quickly up to the troll and extended his hand. "Thank you, Mushbahc. You are a hero."

"No, sir," Mushbahc grinned, shaking his hand heartily. "Just a troll."

The ship was anchored and the passengers were being taken ashore. Gemaine was both nervous and excited; she was going to see an elfin king! How grand! And perhaps even live in this place for the rest of her life. When she saw the shores, she hoped it was so.

Every color was rich and deep and true. Gemaine had never seen such green grass or such vibrant flowers; nor had she ever seen so many brightly attired birds or such elegant and graceful horses.

They were taken by carriage to the palace in the heart of the Isle. The carriage was a beauty in itself, a light and elegant vehicle with sweeping curves and smooth lines, and the passengers hardly felt a bump as they glided easily toward the palace of Élas. The elves smiled and seemed quite cheerful and radiant. The birds sang sweetly and Scarlyn plucked a beautiful exotic flower for Colly. It smelled so lovely and the petals were so soft and silken. It was the loveliest shade of purple the young girl had ever seen and matched her lilac dress perfectly. Colly herself was so amazed by such a sight, she hardly spoke, gazing about her in wonder and acting quite grown up indeed.

After hours of traveling, they had finally arrived. The group gazed up at the palace in amazement-- all but Berinder, who had seen it before. It was surely the most exquisite and lovely palace they had ever seen. The gardens, the trees, the birds and animals, the crystal lakes and small ivory boats, the stone walks and the polished white walls of the palace were purely breathtaking. Even old Freeno paced calmly by Gemaine's side, gazing in wonder at the new sights that danced before his eyes.

The elegant carriage rolled to a stop before the majestic stone steps. Willow trees lined the walk, vibrant flowering shrubs beneath them. Tall, graceful elves walked past the group, nodding and smiling kindly. The air around them was a rich rosy hue, as if the very sun itself was a different shade. And so it could have been. A feeling of pure joy welled up inside Gemaine's breast, and her aging face was beaming with bliss. To live out the last of her days here, on the Isle of Élas, would be the most wonderful experience of her life.

Berinder strode before them, up to the guards at the door. A regal elf, draped in vivid green, approached and bowed his russet head to the wizard. "Greetings, Lord Berinder, and welcome to Élas Isle."

Berinder nodded in return. "Greetings, Anolai. You look well."

"Thank you, friend. I fear that you have just missed my father. He set out for Berea, not seven days hence."

Berinder looked concerned. "All is well, I trust?"

"Here in Élas, it is. But it seems that it is not so in Midgard. The legendary Mazi magician, Kwea Ankuhr, seeks his council at the embassy in Berea concerning a great evil that is stirring."

"Very well, we shall seek Lord Almyn there. Is your sister nearby?"

"Nay. She journeyed with my father to visit her companion, Nehru Tvildar."

"I see. Very well. Anolai, I am leaving this woman here, under the care and protection of your kin. She is Gemaine Brennan, grandmother to Seaghan Jordahn, King of Damor. This is Colly, his sister. They need refuge from the King's uncle, Kermain."

"So I hear. They are most welcome," Anolai smiled kindly at Gemaine. Gemaine smiled at him gratefully in return and bowed her head.

At the prince's bidding, a kindly gathering of lady elves ushered Gemaine and Colly into the sparkling palace. Berinder turned to descend the stairs, but Anolai called to him.

"Berinder!" The wizard stopped and turned to face the elf as he descended a few steps to draw closer. "My Lord Berinder, should you not rest and continue your journey in the morning?"

"We cannot, for we have urgent dealings with your father." Berinder shook his head. As a second thought, he added, "If you would care to join us, Anolai, we may be in need of your aid."

"Very well. I must remain here for a short time, but I shall follow as soon as I may and lend you what service I can." Berinder nodded and turned to stride down the stairs.

And so, the men set out at once to seek Lord Almyn in Berea and the answers to their mysteries.

Chapter Ten

The road was in poor condition, and the carriage tossed the boy and the old man about quite roughly. Kilme had been informing the lad about the history and people of Damor as they traveled, and Seaghan listened intently to the older man, with bright eyes and thoughtful countenance, considering each piece of advice carefully. They had been traveling for several days. The two tried vainly to keep themselves from being jostled too much as they attempted to carry on their conversation.

"What is wrong with these roads?" Seaghan finally asked, his frustration mounting as he pulled himself up from another jarring fall to the floor of the carriage.

"They have been neglected for some time," Kilme replied. "I have heard that Duke Zaris has been reigning these lands as a tyrant. He overtaxes the poor folk and keeps the gold for himself." Kilme sighed. "I have met with many lords from this land, begging me for aid, but I could do nothing."

Seaghan glanced thoughtfully out the window of the carriage, and was met by a most grievous sight. They were riding through the township at the base of the castle now, and Seaghan watched the passing scene with dismay and pain. The roads and ditches were ill kept, mere mud and rock, and full of murky, stinking water. Children, who had been playing near the festering shallows, froze in silence as the grand carriage rolled by them, the youngest of them scurrying frightened for their mothers. The pitiful buildings of the village were in terrible need of repair, many of them quite beyond that need, a wrenching contrast to the prim, modest homes of Cherin. The peasants scurried to drop to their knees before the oncoming team, fear and dread in their thin, bony faces. Most of them were old and haggard, the few younger ones being mostly women or visibly ill. The smell of decay, rot, and disease filled the air and Seaghan sat back in his seat, sickened by sights as well as scents.

The lad was thoughtfully silent for a moment, then looked up at Kilme with fire in his young brown eyes.

"I loved my father, Kilme. But his was a grave and shameful mistake to abandon his country. Fear of my uncle will not keep me from doing the same. I will do all I can to reunite my grandfather's kingdom once more."

"Bravely spoken, my boy. It does my heart good to hear it. I offer you my aid and counsel, such as it is. I shall be proud to bow to your rule. Despite your age, I do believe you have become quite a man." Kilme touched the boy's shoulder and gave him a look of admiration.

Seaghan nodded solemnly and replied, "Thank you, Kilme. You have taught me much these past few days and I hope to continue to learn from you."

Suddenly the road became even and smooth, and Kilme leaned forward to peer from the carriage window.

"It seems Duke Zaris certainly spared no expense on his castle," he said, brusquely.

Seaghan leaned forward as well and was greeted by a most majestic sight. White stone walls rose into the cloudless sky, their gleaming ivory towers catching the sunlight. The wind whipped at sapphire-blue banners bearing gold insignias, and the water in the moat sparkled like millions of tiny crystals. The battlements and lookouts were quite imposing, encrusted with sharp spikes and guarded heavily by archers in sapphire tunics, carrying elfin-made longbows. When the thick line of grand trees parted, the travelers gazed at a massive stone bridge, lined with spearmen in golden amour. As the Duke's carriage approached, the enormous gates began to swing slowly open and the guards raised their spears in salute. The horses, as if knowing they were home, began to trot proudly, lifting their grey legs regally into the air, their hooves ringing cheerfully on the polished cobble.

The carriage passed through the lines of stone-faced guards and into the lush courtyards. Grand trees and lovely flowers basked in the afternoon sunlight, and cool, clear brooks wound serenely through the beautiful gardens. A tall, stately man with balding head and regal manner, descended the marble steps and quickly crossed the cobble-stone paths towards the carriage. Several steps behind him a small crowd of lords and ladies followed, their steps much slower than his and their mood distinctly heavier. The driver eased the carriage to a stop and a footman leapt to the door with a stool. As the footman threw open the carriage door and bowed low, the tall man stopped and bowed as well, saying, "Welcome home, my Lord Zaris. How fared your meeting---" he froze in sudden surprise as an elderly man stepped lightly from the carriage.

The Tale of Tyrfing

"Your Majesty," he drawled mockingly. "What an unexpected surprise." The other lords and ladies brightened and quickened their pace.

"I am certain, Lord Draltin," Kilme replied. "But waste not your honeyed poison on me, for I come with words which you shall find most bitter."

"Indeed?" the malicious lord replied in a forced air of innocent surprise. "And where is Duke Zaris? I trust he did not come to harm while on a peaceful journey to speak with you?"

Kilme ignored Lord Draltin's insinuations and continued. "Zaris is Duke no longer, but sits in the dungeons of Cherin awaiting trial for high treason and attempted harm upon the life of the king."

Lord Draltin's face began to redden in anger, but his voice remained calm and steady as he addressed Kilme once more with sugared words.

"Then I expect you have come to appoint a new Duke over East Damor? May I remind you that I am Zaris' successor."

"I am aware that as High Lord, you were next in line. However, the kingdoms of West and East Damor are to be reunited and your association with Zaris, a traitor, has cost you your position."

"Foolish talk!" hissed Lord Draltin, losing his composed demeanor. "East Damor is mine! You have no right to sit upon the throne!"

"But I do!" cried a youthful voice. Seaghan stepped imperially down from the carriage, never taking his eyes away from the enraged lord. The group behind Lord Draltin stared speechless at this vision in velvety green.

Regaining his composure, Lord Draltin spoke menacingly. "Who is this whelp who dares to claim the throne of Damor?"

Kilme bowed low to the boy and called out loudly, "Announcing his lordship, High King Seaghan, son of Jaykon, son of Tahlon. Long live King Seaghan!" Instantly, the footman dropped to his knee and the guards, who had dismounted, did the same. The silent lords and ladies dropped quickly to their knees as well, leaving only Draltin standing.

"What?!?!" cried Draltin. "Impossible! The entire family was destroyed! I received a message---" He stopped suddenly, but it was too late.

Kilme was outraged.

"Then you have fraternized with Damor's deadliest and most treacherous enemy! Guards! Seize this traitor!"

The horses' clipping stopped and a drow perched upon the back of a chestnut mare shook himself awake to survey the area. It was quite early in the morning; the dew still hung in the air and glistened on the rich green grasses. The sun had yet to peek above the horizon, and the sky was just beginning to lighten. Trees were sparse and tall, with plenty of field land and pastures between them. A gnome and an elderly Mazi sat fully awake on a majestic black stallion, watching the people go by on the road at the foot of the hill. Before them, for miles and miles, as far as the eye could see, stretched a grand and bustling city, its massive walls reaching towards the sky and shielding their eyes from what lay behind.

The Mazi and the drow urged their horses swiftly toward the high city walls, set aflame by the morning sun. Ten barbarians stood guard at the massive city gates, five on each side. A golden-haired, stern-looking elf stepped forward with parchment and quill and addressed them brusquely.

"Each of you must state your name, race, and business in Berea," he commanded.

The drow spoke first. "Phoenix Talrid, drow and wood elf. I and my fellows seek Lord Almyn Ostara at the elfin embassy."

The elf gave him a doubtful look at the mention of his mixed race, but spoke no ill. He nodded toward the magician.

"Kwea Ankuhr, good elf. I am a Mazi magician. I accompany this fine lad to see Lord Almyn." The elf nodded respectfully and glanced down at Krimple.

"Krimple Bumblegorf, gnome," the small man stated matter-of-factly.

The elf nodded and wrote quickly on his parchment. "Enter in peace and stay in peace," he told them, waving them on. His voice was calm and civil, but his tone told them this was just as much a warning as an invitation. The group nodded to him and passed through the heavy gates and into the city.

They walked some way, leading their horses past vendors and merchants, pubs and inns, courtyards and gardens, jesters and dancers. They passed a large grassy field where a giant lounged, then a massive park wherein were gryphons and eagles, pixies and faeries, as well as all manner of woodland creatures. As they strolled by the massive black towers of the shadow elves' embassy, Phoenix's eyes wandered over the iron gates and shadowy courtyards. Near the large doors to the embassy stood a tall, grand, dark tree. Beneath it, Phoenix spied the most beautiful maiden he had ever seen.

Her skin was a soft shade of grey and her long soft curls were of the blackest ebony. A long satin dress fell gracefully over her shoulders, its azure folds forming to her charming figure. Her alluring face was both regal and gentle, and her deep violet eyes spoke volumes. The dainty curves of her exquisite lips curved into a sad pout. Her eyes seemed to be gazing off into the distance; her mind was clearly in some distant land. Phoenix stood captivated by her astonishing beauty until Kwea nudged him sharply.

"The daughter of Baral is certainly lovely, but an unabashed stare is not the most princely of actions, young elf." The Mazi murmured softly.

Startled, Phoenix turned toward the magician. "Baral? The ambassador?"

"Yes, Baral Tvildar. That is his daughter, Nehru."

The Tale of Tyrfing

Phoenix turned to look again, but the beautiful Nehru had vanished. He scanned the dusky courtyard, but could see no sign of the enchanting drow. He continued on, following Kwea toward the shimmering ivory towers of the elfin embassy, but his mind lingered on the lady whose enthralling eyes and unmatched beauty had so won his attention.

The group ascended the sparkling white steps and entered the great halls of the elves of light. An elf, robed in scarlet, greeted them and bowed graciously. He led them down the stone halls enveloped in ivy vines, and into a large, round room. The room was nearly empty, containing only an altar bearing vines, flowers, fruits and candles, as well as a few tall candlesticks and a long bench. Before this bench stood Berinder and Almyn, conversing quietly. As the party entered, the two elders turned toward them and waited silently as they approached.

"I'm glad you've arrived Phoenix. We have a very important matter to discuss," Berinder said earnestly to his apprentice when they had drawn near. He looked to the Mazi. "You are Kwea Ankuhr who seeks Lord Almyn's aid?"

"I am." Kwea replied with a nod.

"I believe I have other guests who share your purpose, friend Kwea," Almyn said calmly. At that moment, a barbarian, an elf and a dwarf entered the room through one of the many side doors. Berinder introduced them. "This is Galayvin, Scarlyn, and Kundin, Lord of Mount Roguk."

"A wood elf and a barbarian," Kwea nodded in mysterious satisfaction. "How fitting. Who else should it be who would destroy the phantom?"

A short time later, they were all seated at a large table, being served a feast of kings. Phoenix turned to Berinder, the only member of the party yet uninformed. "Please tell me of this phantom," he implored.

Berinder beckoned to the Mazi. "Perhaps we should let the one who imprisoned him tell the story," he said.

Everyone turned to the magician and listened intently. He bowed his head to the wizard then spoke softly. "Yes, I shall tell you my story." He spoke to them of the day in Hakik when he had first heard tell of a dark elf necromancer. He spoke of the attack upon himself and his companions that dark night and told them of the goblin who had once been a king of men. Then he spoke of how he had first come face to face with the evil necromancer, Nakasuin.

Chapter Eleven

Year 67 of the Shadow Age, Piyr, Midgard

Upon hearing Krage's tortured tale, Krimple and Kwea decided something must be done about the necromancer, Nakasuin. The other Mazi joined them and the party set out for the castle, guided by the goblin-man. When they reach ed the gloomy place, they found an onyx fortress set upon blackened soil, where no living thing grew. The goblin let out a terrifying screech as he spied his brothers. Their heads were severed and driven onto pikes, their bodies crushed and dismembered, scattered around the grounds beneath the pikes. Kwea and his companions were immediately surrounded by a clattering army of skeletons and goblins. A tense battle between good and evil waged then and the night sky was illuminated by the flash of ice, fire, and lightning.

A skeleton stepped towards Kwea, raising a wicked looking spear above its head. A blast of ice from the magician merely pushed the skeleton back a step. It quickly regained its ground and hurled the spear toward Kwea. The Mazi easily struck the spear off its course with his staff and sent another hard blast of ice at the creature. The skeleton fell back and dropped to its knees, but was not defeated yet. It plunged its bony hand into the black earth and pulled a sword from below the ashen surface. Rattling to its feet, the animated dead lunged towards him, dodging another icy blast and swinging its black blade at the Mazi magician. Kwea barely ducked out of the way, and twisted himself so that he could swing his staff and strike the skeleton's spine just below the skull. The blow was just enough to crack the bones and leave the skull dangling. And yet the skeleton spun around to attack once more. A sharp blast of ice finished the job however, and without its skull, the corpse crumbled into dust at the Mazi's feet.

Kwea had no time to revel in his victory, for a goblin was swinging a crude blade at him and a skeleton was climbing shakily from the ground to join the fray. Filled with battle rage, yet overwhelmingly calm, as was characteristic of his race, Kwea battled ferociously against the spawn surrounding him.

After several moments, Kwea noticed that, though the goblins were easy enough to kill, as soon as he destroyed each skeleton another one rose from the ash riddled ground to take its place. He turned and murmured to a nearby of his brethren.

"Fight on, friend. I shall away and find the master of th e walking dead." The Mazi nodded and turned back to the battle before him, lightning flashing from his gnarled staff, bright enough to blind his foes for but a moment, and give his brother time to vanish. Krimple conjured up a strong vine to ascend the castle's onyx wall and Kwea immediately began to climb it.

Pulling himself through a high window, the magician looked cautiously around. All was silent – deathly silent. He walked carefully and quietly down the dim, shadowy halls. There were no guards or minions walking the cold halls. Likely they had all been sent to do their master's bidding on the grounds below. Kwea crept onward, past piles of broken bones and rotting corpses. Every few paces, a flickering, blue-flamed torch lit the way, surrounded by sharp onyx spikes, creating a sinister and threatening form of architecture.

Finally a voice reached the ears of the Mazi. He froze and listened carefully. He could not make out the words, but the droning hum of the devilish voice spoke of a casting of malefic spell. The Mazi slipped swiftly toward the partially closed door at the end of the dim hall. Peering through the crack, Kwea saw a dimly lit room, aglow with blue torches such as he had seen in the halls. Books, scrolls, and various dusty objects were piled around the room where, in the center, a shadow elf stood before a large book propped on a skeletal pedestal. He held his hands outstretched, palms toward the book, and was repeating a demonic mantra. Unnatural blood dripped from the pages of the book and a fiendish voice was replying to the drow's call.

Kwea lifted his copper hand to his lips and blew softly towards the book. A light, frosty breeze swiftly froze the trickling blood. The murmuring voice from the book shrieked in terror and pain, and the drow whirled about to face his enemy.

"Prepare to die, magician!" he hissed, an evil hate spilling from his abyssal eyes.

But Kwea had different intentions. He had seen a black band bearing strange markings upon the wrist of the drow and a scheme leapt into his mind. He immediately began to search his thoughts for the proper spell, as he and the drow began to circle, their eyes locked.

"Funesto Nex Necis!" the necromancer cried out suddenly. A bolt of green light shot from his fingertips.

"Pellere Morti!" Kwea replied, his light-shield barely deflecting the spell in time.

Again, they continued to circle. Suddenly Kwea stopped. The elf stopped too, and prepared to defend himself against whatever spell the magician would use.

But he was not ready for what the magician had planned.

Kwea held up his hand and his strong voice uttered the words, "Ligo Necetere Relego Aeternitas."

Instantly, Nakasuin clutched at the band on his wrist. His eyes grew wide and he screamed in pain. Desperately, he clawed at the tightening ring. Then, though his face was wrenched in pain, he stood tall and threatening as he quickly spat out his own spell.

"My binding could not be reversed," Kwea told the men who listened keenly to his tale. "But the necromancer was able to counter it, in his own way. I had bound his essence to the anklet in death-- but he managed to alter it into undeath. His malicious spirit is now bound to the band and he is unable to cause any harm on his own. However, he has the ability to control anyone fool enough to wear the band. I could not destroy it, but I was able to hide it deep within a tomb in the mountains of Gamlin. There it remained for many years while I searched for a way to destroy it. But to the pain and despair of many, a grave robber, a shadow elf by the name of Morrana, has discovered it and it is she who has unleashed this demon."

Phoenix clenched his fists and stood. "Let us go now! We must destroy this phantom!" he exclaimed. Galayvin rose also, his hand at his sword, ready to follow Phoenix.

"I'm afraid that is not possible, my boy," Berinder replied calmly. "It is no easy task to destroy a demon."

Galayvin sighed gloomily and resumed his seat, but Phoenix stood firm. "Then we leave Morrana to her doom?" he questioned, angrily.

"No, no" Berinder assured him. "For that would mean the destruction of Piyr as well. No, we shall do something to save the maiden, but not yet. First, Almyn and I have a task for you."

Phoenix's fiery eyes showed the struggle in his heart. Finally deciding to heed the wizard, the passionate lad took his seat. "Very well," he relented. "Where would you have me go?"

"Galayvin and Scarlyn will go with you. I send you to no easy task, for the mines of Kanor are not to be taken lightly."

Galayvin looked at him skeptically. "The mines of Kanor? What sort of place is that?"

"The mines themselves have rarely been entered by any mortal who survived them. You will find the entrance to the mines at the far eastern borders of Damor, north of Kerik."

"And who is this Kanor?" Phoenix asked.

Scarlyn answered him. "He was once a great and formidable giant; a warrior of remarkable strength and power. They say he knocked on the door of a cottage in Damor early one winter. He asked for shelter and was given the barn, for the house could not hold him. He requested food and was brought a meager meal of bread and gruel, for the poor family had little else. He was angry for the lack of fine food and with his bare hands, he destroyed the man's barn and home."

Galayvin grinned at his friend. "Is there anything you don't know?" Scarlyn smiled slightly at him and continued.

"The man had given him all he had and was bitter at the giant's ingratitude. His barn, all his crops, his home, and every one of his animals were destroyed, and winter was on his doorstep. Worse, his wife and two daughters were crushed beneath the rubble. The peasant sought out a wizard of Golondere and begged for vindication. The wizard had in his possession a gem-- the Amort Stone. This was a legendary gem of much power. It brought death to the living and caused the dead to rise and walk again in a state of unrest. To the undead it brought complete destruction. It is unknown why the wizard gave the stone to the peasant, but the giant was never seen again. It is said that he dwells deep within the mines of East Damor, a specter, served by ghouls and the walking dead."

"And it is there that you will find him. I send you to retrieve the Amort Stone. Do not touch the jewel, but carry it in this pouch." Berinder handed Phoenix a leather satchel.

"Then let's be off," Galayvin said, quickly standing again. "We've got a giant to hunt."

"Hear this!" Lord Almyn said quickly. "Kanor is no longer mortal. It will take great skill and comradeship to destroy him. None of you can do this alone. Your companions will be your greatest asset in battling this ghostly warrior."

Berinder nodded in agreement. "The only way to kill an undead," he added, "is to sever the head. This will be quite difficult, considering the giant's size and strength."

"Victory will be ours," Phoenix stated confidently. "We will return as soon as we have the Stone." Spinning on his heels, he strode quickly from the room. Galayvin bowed reverently to the wizard and the elf lord, and swiftly followed the reckless young man. Scarlyn did likewise.

Kwea smiled. "He is young and foolhardy," he said of Phoenix. "But his spirit is strong."

Berinder agreed. "I see great promise in the boy, aside from his impatience and arrogance."

Chapter Twelve

The dust kicked up about Gren's sandals as he ran quickly through the hot streets of Cherin. Most of the inhabitants were at the temple and Gren heard the horn calling them to beseech the Gods for the safety of the soldiers as they hunted the enemy of Damor. A few stragglers bustled past him, parting to give him clearance as he flew toward the guardhouse of the captain. Captain Guresh, Jerril, Mahlon, and Treyvis were inside, pouring over maps of Kerik to plan their route. Gren burst wildly through the door and they looked up, startled.

"Captain! Captain Guresh!" Gren shouted breathlessly.

"What is it, Gren?" Guresh asked, turning apprehensively toward him. Jerril's one eye stared unsettlingly at him, and Mahlon and Treyvis each took a step forward anxiously. The two of them often did things simultaneously, as if they were twins, though it was obvious from their appearances they were not even related, one being dark of hair and skin, the other lightly tanned with ruddy orange hair. But for all that, they did share a seeming similarity, both in eye and carriage, and the fact that they were nearly always seen together had given them an air of inseparableness that permeated their presence enough to make them seem as brothers, even though they shared no real physical attributes.

"I wish to accompany you," Gren panted.

"Has Cleric Saldor declared you well enough?" Guresh asked, unsmiling. He understood Gren's desire to join them, but he could not tolerate someone who would slow them down.

"He has," Gren replied. "He just doesn't know it yet."

"Can you lead us to Jaykon's home?" Guresh asked, attempting to hide his smile.

"I can."

"Very well. We begin there. Jerril, summon the rest of the troops. We leave immediately."

Jerril bowed his nearly bald head and vanished.

"Mahlon, gather the maps and secure them on my horse. Treyvis, send a messenger to Thorahn and alert the king of our plans; then the two of you join us quickly," Guresh ordered.

"Yes sir!" the men hurried to obey their captain. As Treyvis left, another figure darkened the doorway of the guardhouse.

The man was tall and handsome with perfectly tanned skin and rippling muscles. His dark curls fell carelessly to his broad shoulders and his clean-shaven jaw was strong and set. On his left arm he wore a long glove on which was perched a magnificent hawk, brown with a grey-white belly. The bird did not boast the usual hood worn by most hunting hawks, for the cap was not necessary on such a bird. It sat calmly upon the man's arm, watching Gren and Guresh with its tiny black eyes. The man cracked a pearly smile at Guresh.

"Ah! Tridar! Will you be joining us?" the captain asked, returning the smile warmly.

"Of course," the man boomed cheerfully. "It wouldn't be the same without me."

Guresh chuckled and clapped Tridar on the shoulder. "Gren," he said. "This is Tridar, one of my best men."

Tridar grinned. "Well I learned from you, sir."

"This is Gren, our guide from Kerik," Guresh added, gesturing toward Gren.

The men shook hands firmly and nodded in respect towards each other. As Gren pulled back his hand he asked, "Are you a swordsman or an archer?"

Before Tridar could respond, Guresh laughed. "Neither! But he does attract the ladies."

Gren smiled slightly at this and Tridar chuckled. "My friend here does the killing for me," he said. "He is called Drosk. No, my task is words. I am often the negotiator for the captain, should the need arise."

Guresh grinned. "Tridar's honeyed words can convince any enemy give up his sword and enter into a treaty--- and any woman to reveal her jewels." With the last, Guresh added a wink.

"A worthy skill," Gren commented, smiling faintly. "But the enemy we hunt now will get no such favor. Your talent will not be needed against him."

Tridar and Gren locked glances for some moments, each attempting to read the other's mind. Finally the captain spoke solemnly. "Gren is right, Tridar. You are welcome, as always, but we bring only death to our quarry."

"Very well," answered Tridar, turning his eyes from Gren to the captain. "I shall accompany you all the same, Captain." A wide grin spread across Tridar's face as he said this and reflected in the older man's face.

"Very good!" Guresh agreed and turned to Gren. "Shall we set forth then?"

"Yes, let us be swiftly off," Gren nodded.

"Aye, time waits for no man," agreed Tridar with a smile.

Gren passed them both and stepped through the door, adding, "Neither does damnation."

A giant figure, cloaked and hooded, strode tirelessly toward the massive gates of Berea. A sword dangled at his side and a white furkle perched comfortably on his broad shoulder. The elf at the gate stepped forward with his parchment and quill in hand.

"State your name, race, and business in Berea," he commanded.

"Mushbahc. Troll and barbarian blood. I seek Berinder, the wizard."

The elf looked surprised. "Troll and barbarian? I have heard tell of you, and it is an honor to finally lay eyes on you. The furkle is quite the perfect companion for you," he said. "As rare and unique as its master. Enter, friend Mushbahc, and know that Berinder awaits you at the elfin embassy with the elfin lord, Almyn Ostara. Enter in peace and stay in peace." The elf stepped aside and Mushbahc passed through the gates into the city. Shrugging past merchants and traders, the troll made his way steadily toward the white stone towers of the embassy. He was ushered into the same room in which the wizard's apprentice, Phoenix. had first met Lord Almyn. Berinder and Almyn stood as before, only silent and waiting.

"Mushbahc," Berinder addressed him as he drew near. "How fares young Seaghan?"

"He is well," the troll replied. "He has assumed the throne under Kilme's guidance and has already begun to unite Damor. Just before I left, Duke Zaris had been overthrown and imprisoned by the lad's orders, after which Seaghan and Kilme left for Thorahn."

"Excellent," the wizard smiled. "Damor's brighter days have begun."

Mushbahc bowed in reverence to the elfin lord who nodded in return. "Has Phoenix arrived yet?" he asked, turning back to Berinder.

"He was here," the wizard replied. "And he brought the Mazi, Kwea Ankuhr. I sent Phoenix and two others to the Mines of Kanor, by way of giant, to retrieve something for me."

"However," Lord Almyn added gravely. "They should have returned days ago."

"Father," a voice came suddenly from beside them. "I will go and find them." A young elf strode into the room, a majestic white tiger at his heels.

Almyn nodded. "You are welcome travel with Mushbahc."

"I don't need a troll," the prince replied, bitterly. "Elara and I will be fine."

"No," Lord Almyn said sternly. "Mushbahc is being sent to do this task. If you can suppress your arrogance, you may join him."

The prince hesitated for a moment, then turned angrily on his heels and stormed from the room, casting a brooding glance toward Mushbahc.

As he approached a doorway, however, he was met by a lovely elfin maiden.

"Anolai?" she asked sweetly. "What troubles you, brother?"

"Father has taken to consorting with trolls," Anolai replied indignantly.

"If Father trusts him, he must have good reason, dear brother," his sister objected tenderly.

"I trust Father, but I cannot trust the likes of him," Anolai said in disgust, motioning towards the troll who had thrown back his hood. The princess glanced at Mushbahc and immediately their eyes locked. Mushbahc stared shamelessly at the beautiful maiden.

In return, she saw something in the eyes of the monster that caused her heart to quicken. The glance seemed to go unnoticed by Berinder, who was explaining the quest to a barely-heeding troll, but Anolai saw his sister's entrancement.

"Aleya? Do you see something in this demon?" Anolai asked quietly, his tone softened.

"I see a good heart, Anolai," she responded, turning to look at her brother. "Do not be so quick to judge by appearances, sweet brother."

Anolai stiffened. "Have you forgotten the past so easily, sister?"

"Never, Anolai." Aleya quickly and passionately assured him. "But events of the past do not always foretell deeds of the future. His race may be known by their black hearts, but this troll is wholly unusual."

Anolai looked at his sister for a moment then nodded. He strode quickly across the room to his father.

"Father," he started and then stopped. He turned to look Mushbahc in the face. "Forgive my distrust. Elara and I will follow you to Kanor's Mines."

Mushbahc returned his gaze steadily, then turned and walked wordlessly from the room. Anolai glanced at his father apologetically and followed the troll. Aleya watched them leave as she crossed the floor to her father and grasped his hand.

Guresh sat tall and proud on his horse, flanked by Tridar and Gren, his rich emerald cape blowing behind him in the warm breeze. Treyvis and Mahlon rode side by side next to Gren, and Jerril rode unnervingly silent on Tridar's left, Tridar pretending to ignore his presence. A leaf, caught by the wind, fluttered down and landed on the breast of his amour, resting peacefully across his heart. He lifted it up and looked at it as if it could tell him a story.

"Autumn approaches," he stated to the men near him.

As he dropped the leaf to the ground, a scout rode quickly up to him.

"Sire, the trail stops a few miles ahead," he told Guresh breathlessly.

"Stops?" Guresh asked, confused.

"Yes, sire. Vanishes." The scout's horse turned restlessly, and he reigned her in again so that he could face the captain.

Captain Guresh looked crushed. "Then he knows we're tracking him," he said thoughtfully.

"How can he know?" Gren asked, almost angrily.

"There must be a betrayer among us," Guresh said simply. "And I intend to find out who that traitor is."

Murmurs erupted throughout the company, whispers of who could stoop so low and for what reason this individual could betray. Only Guresh, Gren, Tridar, and the ever-present Jerril sat stonily silent on their mounts.

Any attempt Anolai made at conversation was met only by quiet from the troll. They had left the gates of Berea behind three days ago and the elfin prince was becoming impatient with Mushbahc's unrelenting silence. He finally followed wordlessly as well.

After a few days more of traveling, the elf began to sense an evil presence. He looked uneasily around and spoke softly.

"The days and the trees grow darker, the animals are restless, and the birds are quiet. The air seems to thicken with fear and the stench of blood."

For the first time since they had left the city, Mushbahc replied. "We are less than a day's walk from the Uruz Labyrinth. It is the prey of the Guardian you smell."

Anolai looked surprised, though unafraid. "You can navigate the Labyrinth?"

"That and many other unpleasant places. There is only one place in all of Piyr that I have not been. From the wastelands of Nartok to the icy peaks of Srak I have trekked. Stay close within the labyrinth. We will not stop nor rest until we are safely out of it."

Anolai nodded in understanding. "And how did you learn to navigate such a place?" he asked. But Mushbahc said nothing and the elf sighed in defeat.

They continued on in silence until Mushbahc stopped. "We will camp here tonight. It is best to challenge the labyrinth at the start of a new day."

By Sokarjo Stormwillow

The elf nodded and knelt to whisper into the ear of his cat. The ivory feline bounded away and Anolai smiled at Mushbahc. "Elara will bring us a feast tonight. I will gather some dead wood for a fire." Mushbahc nodded and turned to survey the landscape before them.

The land was flat and the dark forest ended abruptly behind them. The soil was black and the ground littered with dead branches and dry bones. Some distance away the forbidding walls of the labyrinth rose into the stormy sky. It seemed that the walls stretched on forever in their solidity, but the troll knew better. From where he stood, he could see the blackened tree with the scorched corpse swinging from its branches and he knew it to be a marker for the entrance. The sky beyond was beginning to darken, and off in the distance Mushbahc could see black clouds boiling and churning, lighted occasionally by the flash of lightning. A low rumble warned him of the impending storm and he looked quickly around for Anolai.

The elf was a stone's throw away, still loading his arms with blackened branches. Mushbahc started towards him, intent on gathering larger wood for a shelter, when a second sound met his ears. He turned to face the labyrinth as he heard a lower, more primal growl. Brave and ferocious as he was, a shiver ran down the troll's spine when he heard the sound. He strode quickly towards the elf, who had heard the growl as well and was frozen in his tracks.

"The beast is on the hunt tonight," Mushbahc told him. "You should call Elara back. Food or no food, it is best that we stay together tonight." The next rumble was from the black clouds flying swiftly towards them. "The heavens will bleed soon. We had best hurry."

Anolai nodded as Mushbahc turned to gather wood. Laying his armload upon the ash-covered ground, Anolai cupped his hands around his mouth. A sharp, clear whistle rang out, rippling on the wind and echoing through the forest nearby. Silence. Anolai looked troubled, but Mushbahc continued to gather dead branches. As a third call died away, Elara finally answered.

Mushbahc looked startled and dropped the wood he had gathered. "That came from the labyrinth..." he said anxiously. A sudden roar alarmed them both. "And the beast is hot on her trail!"

Anolai did not hesitate. Quick as the lightning above their heads, he shot across the black soil towards the wall.

"Wait!" the troll bellowed, snatching up two large branches and following him. The furkle clung to his shoulder as he pounded towards the threatening labyrinth. At the wall, the elf stopped, glancing around, unsure where to go. The troll quickly gained on him, tossed him a branch and shouted, "Light it!" then ran towards the corpse trembling in the stormy gusts. His steps slowed as he reached it and he paused to light his torch. Stuffing the flint back into his pouch, he strode quickly to the narrow entrance behind the tree. As he stepped through the gap, Mushbahc drew his claymore. Behind him, Anolai unsheathed his sword and followed him.

"Stay close and be watchful," Mushbahc warned him. The two crept quickly and quietly, zigzagging through the stony maze as the sky grew steadily darker.

Suddenly a gust of wind snuffed both torches and the rain began to pour. Mushbahc looked wildly around for the elf, but could see him nowhere.

"Anolai!" he shouted, and his call was answered by a roar of a beast on the hunt.

Mushbahc began to run.

Chapter Thirteen

The small army had been traveling for days. Their horses were tired and filthy and their food was running low. But their spirits could not be dampened and they pushed on, relentless and strong. Their hatred for their quarry and their enthusiasm about their new young king kept them going. Change was in the air and it seemed each man felt it.

At the front of the line rode Captain Guresh and Gren. Towards late afternoon, a man rode up beside the captain with a hawk upon his arm. "So where is this village of yours, Gren?" he asked amiably.

"Tirish is a day's ride from here," Gren responded gravely, still pondering the betrayal that seemed to be lurking within the ranks.

"And a good thing, too," added Guresh. "We need supplies."

"Captain, the horses need to rest," Tridar said. "As do the men. We should make camp now. I'd like to send Drosk out for food."

Guresh turned and looked back at the men behind him. They looked blithe enough, but Tridar was right; they were exhausted. Guresh turned back to him and nodded. "Very well, Tridar. Give the signal to set up camp. Gren and I will have a look around." Tridar nodded as the two men rode off.

The daylight faded quickly and the night sky was dark with angry clouds before Gren and Guresh returned. They walked, silent and weary, toward their tents, side by side at the edge of camp.

Guresh suddenly held up his hand and motioned for Gren to be still. The two men crouched behind a tent as a figure emerged from another one nearby. The figure seemed not to sense them as it crept towards the forest. Then it stopped and looked around. The men stifled a gasp, but the large goblin did not hear them and dashed into the oak wood looming dark against the night sky. Guresh gestured to Gren to follow and whispered, "They usually travel in packs."

The men peeked into Tridar's tent, fearing for his life. Tridar sat, well and whole, at a table lit by a small lantern. A hooded hawk sat on a perch to his left. An empty pouch lay on the table and he was stacking gold coins and muttering under his breath, a greedy look upon his face.

Enraged, Gren leapt into the tent and caught Tridar across the face with his fist.

"What the--?!?!" Tridar exclaimed just before Gren delivered his blow. He was sent tumbling backward across the floor of the tent and the hawk flapped its wings and screeched. The coins flew in all directions as Guresh swept them angrily from the table.

"How long have you been taking money from goblins?" Guresh demanded.

"I don't know what you're talking about," Tridar seethed, wiping blood from his lip.

"We saw the vermin leaving your tent," Gren spat angrily.

"And your hawk seems to have lost his white underbelly," Guresh observed. And so it had. The entire bird was a rich brown.

"He's dirty," Tridar retorted, spitting blood onto the ground. "And I know nothing of goblins."

Gren clenched his fists. "Who does he work for, Tridar? Who are you taking bribes from?"

Tridar moved to draw his sword, but Guresh was swifter. His blade flashed at Tridar's throat and he fell back onto the ground. Guresh held his sword to the man's face and their eyes met.

"Who does he work for?" Guresh growled menacingly as lightning reflected the fire in his eyes.

Lightening flashed again and Anolai winced as he heard the crunch of bones beneath his feet. Even in the darkness, the keen-eyed elf saw shadows bending and pulsing around him. The restless spirits of slain innocents whispered ghostly warnings to him in a speech he did not know. It was the language of the dead, unintelligible to any living soul save for necromancers, who learn its idiom. Each unearthly murmur sent shivers of fear down the spine of the prince of light. He stumbled once and instantly the ground began to shift as if alive. Blood chilling screams of tortured souls fell upon his ears, seemingly from below the soil. He scrambled to his feet and began to run.

A brilliant flash of lightning lit up the angry faces of the warriors. Filthy from the long day, they looked quite wild as they noisily surrounded their leader. Guresh raised his hands for silence.

"We have a traitor in our midst!" he shouted above the low rumbling of the thunder.

Angry murmurs flitted quickly through the rough crowd.

The Tale of Tyrfing

"This man has been accepting bribes from the enemy, carried to him by goblin kind."

More muttering coursed through the ranks.

"And he has sent word to our prey of our moves... by way of hawk."

Shocked gasps erupted through the crowd as Gren dragged Tridar, bound and gagged, to the center of the circle and forced him to his knees. Gren held his sword to the deceiver's throat.

"Men of Damor!" Guresh called out. "What should be the traitor's punishment?"

Cries for death exploded into the chill night air, challenged only by the rumbling of thunder.

Mushbahc brushed past the dead bodies littering the floor. He thought he must be drawing near to the center of the labyrinth, though in the darkness it was difficult to be certain. He could smell fresh blood, though his senses told him it was that of an animal, not an elf. He still feared the worst and continued searching anxiously for his missing companion.

Suddenly, he tripped over something in the darkness and landed on his side. He sniffed as he sat up. A flash of lightning revealed what his nose had already known. A gazelle lay stiff in fresh blood on the floor of the maze. Its neck bore tooth marks and paw prints surrounded the animal. Elara had made her kill, though what drew her to the labyrinth, the troll could not guess.

He had not long to think on it either, for the air was suddenly filled with a fearsome roar and Mushbahc could tell the beast was close--very close.

"Kill him!"

"Death to the traitor!"

"Sever his head!"

Guresh held up his arms to silence the vengeful throng. Lightning flashed again and rain began to dance with earth and sky.

"Men of Damor!" he shouted again. The men held their tongues but shot looks of hatred and disgust at the enraged Tridar. "Let the traitor speak his last words."

Gren pulled the scarf down that bound Tridar's mouth. Even the thunder was still in anticipation of the turncoat's words.

After an angry pause, Tridar spoke, his voice steady and strong. "If my sentence is death, then so be it. I bow my head to the blade and so die with honor."

"There is no honor for the man who dies a traitor," Gren declared.

"Then know this," Tridar said, his face losing none of its anger and hatred. "Kermain has already left Tirish in ruin. The citizens are dead and the village burned. By heeding me, you have killed them all."

Gren struck Tridar across the face, knocking him to the ground. Guresh held up his hand and pulled Tridar back to his knees. "I believe there's more," he told Gren.

"You're right, old man," Tridar said, spitting blood onto the wet grass. "Kermain's forces have grown. The orcs have joined him, as have most of the trolls and many drow. Most of his forces are traveling under the leadership of a drow named Slythe to retrieve a magical weapon from a dragon's lair."

"And Kermain himself?" Guresh asked, impatiently.

"He plans to visit Cherin while we are away and remove young Seaghan from the throne."

Guresh looked at Tridar calmly. After a long pause, Tridar met his gaze. "I have told you all I know," he said; his voice had softened and his deep brown eyes searched the expressionless face of his former mentor. "Forgive me?" he whispered hoarsely. Guresh's face did not change. He looked up at Gren who nodded once.

"You die a repentant traitor," Gren declared, raising his sword. "But a traitor nonetheless!"

The thunder cracked and the lightning crashed across the sky as Gren's blade found its mark.

Anolai stood still and breathless against a wall as the storm raged overhead. He could hear heavy breathing from around the corner to his left and pounding steps signaled the approach of a giant. The elf held his breath and closed his eyes.

The footsteps passed by and faded away.

Anolai relaxed and opened his eyes. To his right, a twig snapped. "Elara?" he whispered.

A dreadful roar echoed through the labyrinth and a brilliant flash revealed a monster instead.

Black hooves shone in the long flash of light, coarse black hair ran the length of its legs, and its hairless, perfectly toned torso gleamed like bronze. The beast's broad shoulders and powerful arms were covered in strange black markings and it sported a chain of gold around its neck. Its hideous face was truly terrifying, shaped as a monstrous bull's and crowned with two enormous black horns. The Minotaur's eyes flashed red and it roared once more as Anolai braced himself to fight the demon.

The brute lunged and Anolai leapt aside, swinging his blade down across the monster's arm and shoulder. The Minotaur roared in pain and anger and turned on the elf.

Suddenly, a small white, furry creature leapt through the air, plunging its teeth into the monster's fleshy neck. Anolai stepped back, but the beast clutched the tiny creature and flung it hard against the wall of the labyrinth.

The Tale of Tyrfing

Dragyn fell to the floor of the labyrinth, limp. The elf braced himself once more for a battle as the Minotaur turned to face him.

An angry roar echoed through the labyrinth and the massive creature moaned deeply, falling face down with a deafening thud. Behind it stood a troll, a huge stone in his hands.

Dropping the rock and scooping the furkle into his huge hands, Mushbahc shouted above the storm. "Come on!" Anolai nodded then paused and raised his sword above the beast's head.

"No!" Mushbahc shouted, grasping the elf's arm in an iron-like grip. "Just come!"

Anolai glared at the troll, but followed, leaving the Minotaur unconscious on the floor of the maze. His curiosity over the troll's actions vanished for the time being, as a great white tiger came bounding towards him, covered in blood.

"Elara!" Anolai shouted and wrapped his arms around her as she licked his face.

"Is she hurt?" Mushbahc asked.

"No," Anolai replied. "This is not her blood."

"Then let us leave this place at once, before the guardian awakens."

Anolai and Elara followed Mushbahc swiftly as he led them from the deadly labyrinth.

Chapter Fourteen

The rising sun shone bright, red and golden onto the rain-soaked earth, a sharp contrast to the previous night. Soldiers moved slowly through camp, taking down the tents and scattering the ashes from the sodden fires. A small band of men shoveled dirt onto a fresh grave and in the air hung a silent solemnity.

Unnoticed by any other, a thin, wiry man crept stealthily to Tridar's tent. Stepping cautiously inside, he saw that all was left as it had been the night previous, the traitor's gold remaining scattered across the ground, even the brown hawk sat silently atop its perch. As quickly as his long, greedy fingers could scoop together the shimmering coins, the man filled a large saddlebag, taking no time to filter out the grass and clumps of still bloody dirt. When he had satisfied himself that he had salvaged all the gold, he slipped quietly and unseen from the camp, leading a brown mare into the damp forest.

Guresh, Gren, Mahlon, and Treyvis rode cautiously through the muddy fields toward Tirish. They had left by midnight and a few hours after sunrise, the four rode into the tiny village.

The humble huts were burned to the ground, dead men's bodies dotted the street, and the smell of decay hung in the air. The four riders stared in dismay at the ruins.

A sound startled them and they turned to see an old man shuffling towards them through the rubble. He looked up at them with dismal and somnolent eyes.

"Are you hurt, Conac?" Gren asked anxiously as he leapt from his horse and rushed to the old man's side.

"Gren... oh, dear boy... you've come back... No... I am not hurt... not by the weapons of men at least," the dried voice replied weakly.

Mahlon leapt from his horse and ran to aid Gren. The two men led Conac to Guresh and Treyvis who had also dismounted.

"Are you the only survivor?" Guresh asked.

"I am. If only the Gods had sent you..." his voice trailed off and he sighed wearily. "My son hid me in a ditch. He was slain... I was never found." He pointed a shaking, bony finger at the ashen center of the village. "The women and children were locked inside the temple. I could hear the screams of my grandchildren as they set the blaze. I could do nothing to save them."

Gren's face blazed with anger then paled in anguish as he heard Conac's story. Guresh shook his head sadly. "We might have arrived in time had I not heeded Tridar's advice. He was right. I killed them all."

Gren turned to him, now stone-faced. "You could not have known. Tridar deceived us all. But he paid his price. Now it is time for Kermain to pay his."

Guresh nodded. "Bring Conac and let us ride quickly back to camp. I have a plan."

Anolai was hungry and tired, but he dared not voice his complaints. The troll pushed him on, with Elara close behind, as they moved quickly through East Damor's impoverished land. The Mines of Kanor were close.

After several hours, they stopped at a murky creek to wash away the blood and dust from the labyrinth. Dragyn, still weak, but alive, lapped slowly at the cool water.

Anolai had been troubled by something and when he had washed himself, he finally asked his question.

"Why did you allow the demon to live?"

Mushbahc did not reply until he had finished strapping on the last of his amour and weapons over his leather acton. Anolai waited silently. Finally Mushbahc spoke, firmly but softly.

"You are a prince of light. It may be difficult for you to understand."

Anolai did not speak, but waited for him to continue.

"There is good, and there is evil. They are separate forces, but one cannot exist without the other. They define each other. My father, Grimfar, was a troll--- my mother, Sitka, was a barbarian. I am both light and dark, good and evil. I was raised in Srak, but my father took me all over Piyr and trained me to hunt, to track, and to guide. He died at the hands of the Minotaur."

"Then you have a right to kill the monster."

"No!" Mushbahc took two long strides up the bank and turned back to the elf. "Not for all the wealth or power in Piyr would I strike that beast down. Listen to me. Speak of this to no one, not even the empty darkness." Mushbahc hesitated and the elf came closer. "The labyrinth holds more

The Tale of Tyrfing

than a deadly monster," he said quietly. "Secrets lie hidden there that, if uncovered, would destroy Piyr completely. The Minotaur guards those secrets from the world. Without the demon, all of damnation would be upon us."

The troll turned on his heel and strode quickly away. Anolai stared thoughtfully after him. "That's all you had to say," he muttered. Then a thought crossed his mind. "Mushbahc!"

The troll stopped and let the elf catch up.

"If you knew about the Minotaur, why did we enter the labyrinth at all? I was almost killed!"

Mushbahc flashed a sharp-toothed grin. "Were you scared, little elf? I thought you didn't need a troll--- you and Elara were fine, right?"

Anolai glared after the troll then followed him, retorting, "I almost had him, you know. If you hadn't gone bashing him with a rock, I would have..."

"Killed him?" Mushbahc asked with a grin. "I was doing you a favor, little elf."

"Stop calling me that!" Anolai raged.

Several days passed, but Anolai and Mushbahc were no longer traveling in sullen silence. They argued constantly and fought over everything. Their bickering was good-natured enough, however, and bonds of friendship grew ever stronger. At last their journey was ending and they spied the stony, barren entrance to the mines.

Beside the shadowed hole sat a figure, cloaked in green and looking quite annoyed and impatient. The troll and the elf looked at each other anxiously, and then started down the hillside. The barbarian stood up to pace and saw them. He began waving his arms frantically, as if worried they might miss the gaping cave and run right passed. Mushbahc and Anolai slowed their pace and strode up to Galayvin.

"Where's Phoenix?" Mushbahc demanded to know.

"Inside, the arrogant fool," Galayvin replied bitterly.

"Alone?!?"

"No, my friend Scarlyn, the wood elf, is inside as well." The barbarian added.

"Why did you not follow?" Anolai asked crossly.

"Because Phoenix insisted he could defeat Kanor alone because he's a wizard's apprentice, and he set up a barrier and only Scarlyn was able to cross it!" Galayvin retorted.

Anolai nodded and strode quickly toward the entrance. Galayvin extended his hand toward Mushbahc and the troll shook it firmly.

"Glad you're both here," Galayvin said, his voice calmer.

Mushbahc nodded and grinned. "You should be glad I could keep the elf alive long enough to get him here. He's been determined to get himself killed since we left Berea."

Anolai shot the troll a look of disdain and Galayvin burst into laughter.

"You should be glad I decided to come along," Anolai retorted as the two came up behind him. "The way is clear."

Mushbahc grinned and walked forward. But as he began to step inside, he seemed to hit a wall and fell backwards, holding his arm.

"Oh, pardon me," said Anolai smugly as his hands glowed golden. He waved them slowly before the entrance. "Now the way is clear." Mushbahc growled, but Galayvin laughed, slapped the troll on the back, and marched into the mine. Mushbahc and Anolai followed, leaving Elara and Dragyn, who had refused to enter the mines, to wait outside.

Within the cave, the three men lit their torches and began to trek deep into the mountain. After some time of shuffling through the cold, close, dark tunnels, the trio came to an old wooden door covered in strange, otherworldly markings. Galayvin pushed through the creaking door and they emerged into an enormous cavern. The ceiling was high enough for a giant to walk easily, and the walls seemed to extend forever. The three men stood on a rocky shore looking out over cold, black water. Nearby, a longboat was tied to a stone. The icy water lapped up against the sides of the boat, and save for the waves, there was no other sound.

Wordlessly, Mushbahc signaled the other two to follow and they climbed aboard the boat. Without warning, the rope slipped free and the longboat slipped into the water. Startled, the men looked around for oars, but there were none. The boat seemed to be guiding itself. Unable to do anything else, the trio sat still and alert, waiting to see where the barge would take them.

Kilme walked briskly through the palace's bright, stone halls toward the royal gardens. Nearing the large wooden door, he passed an elderly stonemason who bowed low, his tools in hand.

"Where is Seaghan?" Kilme asked.

"His Majesty is in the garden, my lord," the worker replied.

"Have you finished?"

"Yes, my lord," and he bowed again.

"Very good. Collect your payment from the treasury."

"Yes, my lord. Thank you, my lord," and with a third bow, the worker vanished.

Kilme stepped from the hall into the palace gardens and breathed deeply. A smile crept across the old man's face and he paused to look around.

The Tale of Tyrfing

The days were becoming cooler now, but many brilliant flowers were still in bloom. Every color of the rainbow danced among lush green leaves and feathery ferns. The sky was blue and wispy white clouds sailed happily across the azure expanse. Scattered throughout this vista were statues--some of warriors, some of maidens, some of horses, and some of other animals. All were well-kept memorials to great kings, beautiful queens, and strong champions.

Seaghan was standing before the newest addition to the garden. A beautiful likeness of a woman from Kerik now stood among the deep blue petals of the forget-me-not. Beneath her was written an epitaph:

In Memory Of

Jaykon Jordahn, son of High King Tahlon
His Lovely Wife, Traida Brennan, of Kerik
And Their Four Young Sons
Aelfric, Conary, Elwen, and Keenan

Every Day Is a Gift

"My mother loved forget-me-not," the youth whispered.

Kilme approached and laid a weathered hand softly on the boy's shoulder. Unshed tears glistened in Seaghan's eyes, but did not fall. For a long, silent moment, they stood there, these two men. One was old and one young, yet they had both seen so much death and suffering. One was in the winter of his years, the other in the flower of youth, yet both bore the heavy load of crown and kingdom. And here they stood, side by side; an old, dying king and a new, young one; two men whose lives had been cruelly touched by the grim shadow of death.

After some time, Seaghan spoke, eyes still on the memorial. "It is a test," he said softly. Kilme listened, motionless. "My life, from birth to this day, has all been to test me; to strengthen my will and my character. Many times I have failed, Kilme --- many times I have fallen and shown weakness. But there is strength of will from my grandfather within me, and the love of my mother gives me hope. I am no longer a boy, but a man, and I must do a man's work." Seaghan looked up at Kilme. "The blood of my uncle should stain my hands, and mine only. He has murdered his own flesh --- it is fitting that his own flesh should strike the death blow. I will send word to Captain Guresh to bring Kermain back here alive. I must avenge my father's death, as well as my grandfather's. Only by this act will my family's honor be restored."

By Sokarjo Stormwillow

Kilme stood thoughtfully silent for a moment. "Then let it be so. You are wise, my son, even in youth," Kilme nodded. "The death blow should be yours, and I would be honored if you would use my old sword. It once gave Kermain a wound on his face. Yet it failed to save the King. It would please me a great deal for you to use it to finish the work."

Seaghan nodded and turned back to the statue. They were silent for a moment, then Seaghan spoke.

"Every day," he whispered. "Every day is a gift."

Chapter Fifteen

A weasel-like man stood before the tent of the leader of an army. He was nervous and trembled slightly, but retained an air of greedy pride, which gave him the utmost confidence of being received warmly. Beneath his muddy cloak, long, slender fingers clutched a large pouch filled with stolen gold.

A captain approached. "His Majesty will see you now," he said, beckoning the man forward.

With quick arrogance and certainty, the weasel stepped forward, entering the grey tent readily. He stood before a tall, cruel looking man whose scarred face and bitter eyes struck enough fear into the weasel's heart as to make him tremble more visibly, though his haughty pride and greed gave him the courage to speak clearly and strongly.

"Greetings, oh great king," he began, filling his words with as much honey as he could muster. "I am Hahmel and I bring you news from the camp of Captain Guresh." He paused a moment, waiting for encouragement to continue. Kermain merely stared wordlessly at him and after a slight, awkward moment, he continued.

"Your spy, the great and noble Tridar, has been found out, oh gracious lord. He was last night executed by Captain Guresh himself, at the hands of Gren Brennan, the brother by marriage of your late broth-"

"Speak not that name!" Kermain rose in exploding fury, instantly silencing the turncoat, who immediately bowed low, letting slip, by sheer accident, the purse of gold he carried. The bag jingled as it landed, several pieces of bloodied gold sliding out of the mouth and into full view of Kermain and his guards.

Hahmel's eyes widened, but he kept his bow low and waited in fear for Kermain's next words. A long silence followed, disturbed only by the increasingly heavy breathing of the trembling Hahmel. Finally, Kermain's low voice issued an order.

"Kill him."

The weasel was led screaming in terror from the tent.

The horse's hooves pounded the turf as the rider flew on through Kerik. He was beaten and bruised and his amour was missing. He wore only his tunic and breeches and carried no flag or weapons. To ride thus unarmed and carrying no messenger's flag was dangerous and for this reason had he been robbed. He had left his home with food and clothing and the flag of his dear country to bear him safely to his destination. Now he was stripped and injured and weak with hunger and thirst. His horse had begun to froth at the mouth and he knew he had very little time to reach his mark.

Suddenly he breached a hill and rode straight into the midst of a small army. A shout went up from the men and their leader rode swiftly to the place where the horse and rider had fallen. The horse was dead.

The rider, mercifully, was not. He lay on his back beside the horse, unable to move from weakness. Guresh leapt from his horse and lifted the man's head.

"Speak lad! Who has assaulted you thus and from whom do you run?" he demanded, concerned.

The man replied weakly. "I am Setanta, messenger of King Seaghan of Damor. I have been sent with word to Captain Guresh."

"Then speak, for I am he!"

"His Majesty -- King Seaghan – requests that you bring the traitor back alive – so that he may deliver the death blow himself."

"And who has dared rob and strike a messenger?" Guresh demanded angrily.

"He whom King Seaghan wishes dead," the messenger said hoarsely.

Guresh rose as three soldiers lifted the injured man and carried him to a nearby wagon to be mended. Clenching his fists, he turned angrily to face Gren who had ridden up behind him. "He is truly a scoundrel to thus harm a courier. Not even the lowest vermin would do so. Our new king wants him alive--- it shall be a difficulty to catch him, let alone to take the fiend prisoner."

"Yet we must do so, and quickly. Kermain will have quickened his pace," Gren replied.

"Then we must quicken ours," Guresh answered, mounting his horse. "Jerril!" Turning to Gren he spoke as the one-eyed man rode up beside him. "We will leave the wagons to travel at their own pace." He turned to Jerril, who had heard the comment. "See that the drivers are armed and leave two men as a convoy for each wagon. Then join me immediately." Jerril nodded and turned his horse. "The rest of us will make hast to our king," Guresh added. Gren nodded in approval and the men spurred their mounts on, leading the other horsemen on the chase.

Mushbahc, Galayvin and Anolai scanned the surface of the dark waters for any sign of their two missing comrades. The chilly cave air seemed to seep through their leather garments and slip its icy fingers across their skin.

Suddenly, Galayvin spied a flash of glittering scales and the flick of a large fish's tail. Long auburn locks told him what he saw.

"A mermaid!" he gasped.

"Don't look into her eyes!" Mushbahc quickly warned. Galayvin hastily turned his head away. Mushbahc looked at Anolai and Galayvin as he added, "Your races cannot look into the eyes of a mermaid, or you will be lost forever. I cannot save you once they have you."

The two nodded in understanding.

Galayvin looked painfully at Mushbahc.

But the barbarian had guessed Scarlyn's fate too soon, for a moment later they were hailed by the voice of the elf.

"Galayvin!"

Galayvin saw his friend perched precariously on the tip of a jagged rock protruding from the chilly waves. As if obeying their wishes, the boat turned aside and glided towards Scarlyn. At the rock, the mermaids, angry at the impending loss of their prey, splashed their fins violently at the intruders. But a growl from the troll sent them scurrying away like frightened minnows. Scarlyn leapt gracefully into the longboat and it immediately resumed its mysterious course.

"What happened?" Galayvin asked his friend.

"I was not aware there were mermaids lurking in these waters," Scarlyn replied, in his usual calm tone. "I heard a whisper and looked down. She almost had me, but for the stone my father gave to me before we left."

A glance at the wood elf's chest revealed a thin chain of mithril bearing a single stone that seemed to give off an iridescent gilded glow.

"A golden bloodstone!" Anolai exclaimed.

"Yes," the wood elf nodded. "My father received it from Lord Almyn when he made a journey to Élas Isle."

"What was it your father did to earn such a prize?" Anolai asked in unbridled curiosity.

"He found something Lord Almyn had lost," Scarlyn replied and was silent. His answer was vague and his eyes revealed nothing, and the others did not press him further.

Indeed, they were all silent as the barge slid smoothly over the dark and frigid waters. They kept their eyes averted from the shadowy depths, but searched the rippling surface ahead for land. After some time, that land appeared. A black, rocky shore much like the first awaited their arrival. The boat beached itself and held quite still as the four climbed ashore.

Suddenly, a sinister figure appeared beside them. Cloaked in black rags and carrying an onyx sword, the ghoul's very presence reeked of death and decay. Its face was hidden in shadow, but two eyes glowed red from the depths of its tattered hood, and a hellish voice spoke from beneath the fringes of black.

"You seek a drow," it hissed.

Mushbahc stepped swiftly forward, placing himself between his companions and the menacing specter. "Where is he, demon?" he growled.

"He is the prisoner of Lord Kanor. As are you."

Immediately, shackles rose from the ground, summoned by a wordless gesture from the ghoul, and bound their wrists and ankles. More spectral figures appeared and each captive was hauled away by two of the silent phantoms.

"What are these foul creatures?" Galayvin demanded, struggling against the iron grip of the skeletal fingers.

"Draznahks," Mushbahc replied. "We have no choice but to let them lead us where they will."

The ghouls had no legs, floating instead through the air, seemingly carried on thin, cold mists. They drug their prisoners along rocky tunnels, down cold stone stairs and through heaps of brittle bones, wrenching them viciously if they struggled. On occasion they passed a gap carved into the wall of the cavern. Within these holes, trapped behind rusty iron bars, were dozens of vile creatures who crawled as animals, but had forms similar to that of deformed men. The loathsome creatures were a pale, sickly grey and their lidless eyes glowed red. They flicked their long forked tongues in and out like lizards, and scratched the rocks and bars with their bony claws.

"And what are those?" Anolai questioned the troll.

"I have never seen their like before," Mushbahc answered, then grunted as one of the Draznahks struck the back of his head with the hilt of its sword.

Presently, they arrived in an enormous hall, wherein stood a grand feasting table and a massive fireplace. No food was there, however, in the cobweb coated dishes, and the fire that blazed in the hearth was foul and green and provided no warmth. At one end of the table stood a tall pole and from this stake hung the flaccid body of Phoenix, beaten and tortured, though clinging still to life.

At the opposite end of the bench sat a horrifying figure, more deplorable far than the Draznahks. He was skeletal, but his entire form was a glowing

The Tale of Tyrfing

dull green and his eyes blazed red. He wore a strange amour made of an unearthly material and which shimmered harsh cobalt in the ghastly firelight. Hanging from his side was a mystical sword, which appeared to be dripping with a never-ending flow of blood. The blood ran down the sharp blade of the sword, but vanished before it hit the floor. Seeing the hideous surround, the four brave hostages shuddered with a gripping fear.

Mushbahc felt an uncommonly strong desire to run to Phoenix's side when he saw the pained look on the drow's face. The drow himself felt his heart break when he saw the group arrive. He shot an agonized look at Galayvin and opened his mouth as if to speak, but could only gape and moan.

The four new arrivals were forced to their knees as Kanor rose from his chair. The monstrous ghoul stood as tall as any giant, his massive form towering above them all. The sword at his waist continued to drip as he advanced toward them. A few steps away, he stopped.

"What have you come to take from me?" he asked, and his voice was like none other any of them had heard. It was low and menacing, yet hissed shrilly in their ears. It sent pangs of torture to their temples and made their skulls throb.

Galayvin, Anolai and Mushbahc groaned, their heads swiveled dangerously on their necks and they seemed to have lost all ability to think. The pain was so great, they could not respond. Phoenix also was struck with agony and cried out in pain. Only Scarlyn seemed to posses the ability to speak, though he too was in a great deal of distress.

"We have come for the Amort Stone!" the elf cried bravely.

"It is mine!" screeched the ghost of Kanor.

The ground beneath them began to heave and rumble and rocks crumbled from the ceiling. The three others fell to the ground howling in pain, their shackled hands reaching vainly for their temples, but Scarlyn remained on his knees, though he was in anguish. At that moment, the stone around his neck began to glow and flicker. Scarlyn immediately realized that the pain had subsided and though it remained, it was no more than a dull throb. He murmured words in an elfin tongue and the shackles shattered from around his wrists. Instantly, the elf leapt to his feet and drew his sword. The elf-made blade began to burn with a golden light. Still murmuring the enchanted words, Scarlyn began to circle round the hellish demon. Kanor followed his steps and his eyes blazed in anger.

Two of the Draznahks shrieked towards him, their onyx blades raised. The wood elf's hands gleamed gold. "Fensum Lemures!" he cried, and as he said this, he flung his hand toward them. Blasts of yellow light hurtled towards them and they screamed in terror. Wreathed in sacred flame, the two ghouls swept shrieking from the hall.

The other ghouls vanished in fear at the sight of this unknown power. Scarlyn's eyes glowed with an ethereal golden light. Kanor grinned maliciously. The ghost drew his sword from its scabbard and instantly the blade was engulfed in crimson flames.

"Now you shall die," Kanor snarled menacingly.

Scarlyn did not reply. Kanor pounded towards him and swung his colossal blade at the elf. Leaping swiftly aside, Scarlyn shouted, "Telum Extorris!" and the flaming sword sputtered. It did not die however, and Scarlyn ducked just in time to avoid a second scorching swing.

The effect Kanor's voice had had upon his companions was lifting and Scarlyn shouted another enchantment.

"Rupi Vinculum!" At the words, the shackles binding their ankles and wrists shattered. Mushbahc instantly drew his broadsword and lunged at Kanor, roaring. The startled ghost spun around and struck the troll, sending him flying.

But it was just the break the others needed. Scarlyn shouted "Telum Extorris!" once more. Because the master of the sword was distracted, the flame immediately vanished. At the same instant, Anolai and Scarlyn slammed their swords into each of the ghoul's kneecaps, causing Kanor to crash to the floor. Galayvin leapt onto the massive specter's back and swung his claymore ferociously, severing the ghost's head. With a low moan and a horrible shriek, the spirit of Kanor shattered into hundreds of tiny pieces, the blast slamming with brute force into the walls of the cavern. The men were tossed across the giant room, tumbling over each other.

Immediately the mines began to crumble and give way. Mushbahc leapt to his feet and sheathed his sword as he sprinted to the drow's side. He slashed the ropes with his dagger and lifted the unconscious Phoenix's tortured body onto his back. Turning to the others, who were quickly collecting themselves from the quaking floor, he boomed, "Get out of here!"

Galayvin and Scarlyn fled towards the opening, dodging falling rocks. Anolai ran instead to where Kanor's head had fallen, the only portion of the spirit that had not exploded into dust. Kanor's lidless eyes had ceased to glow. From the ghoul's helmet, Anolai pried a large blood red stone with his sword. Snatching a leather satchel from his side, he slid the gem into it, being careful not to touch the evil jewel. Quickly he followed Mushbahc and the others through the mouth of the hall. The group tore down the tunnels towards the black lagoon. Behind them they heard hideous screeching as the hell-hounds, released from their iron prisons, gave chase. All around them fell large boulders and sharp rocks.

Scarlyn shouted another enchantment and a bright golden light spread itself like a mantle above their heads. Each rock that struck the light was shattered into dust, but the light began to fade quickly. Finally, the company reached the rocky shore, where the magical boat sat waiting. As soon as they were all inside, the long boat turned and glided across the water. As if sensing the urgency, the barge picked up speed quickly and barely seemed to touch the waves. Amidst the roaring of the cavern's collapse, they heard melancholy sobs from the mermaids. The men stared at each other to resist looking into the murky water. Phoenix lay in the troll's strong arms, appearing almost lifeless.

As the group leapt from the longboat, it vanished as if it had never been. Without so much as a glance behind them, the band raced towards the dimming ray of light ahead.

Chapter Sixteen

Golden sunlight streamed in through the plated window, casting criss-crossed ribbons of shadows onto the bed. The melodies of birds filtered into the room, and from below the window came the bustle and clatter of a city awakening. A lovely elfin maiden slipped into the room through the partially opened door. Her copper locks fell softly onto slender shoulders and her velvety green eyes sparkled from beneath long lashes. A gentle smile played about her lips and her cheeks were flushed and rosy. She slipped quietly up to the bed and glanced sweetly down at its slumbering occupant.

Phoenix had bandages round his chest and sides, and salves on his arms and legs. He lay peacefully on a feather pillow, covered with a light sheet. As the maiden glided softly up to the bedside, the drow began to stir and waken. Slowly, his eyes fluttered open and his gaze fell upon the enchanting face of the elf.

"Good morning," she said softly. "I am Aleya Ostara. You are safe in Berea."

"How did I get here?" he moaned weakly.

"Mushbahc carried you from the mines."

"The mines... I don't... the last thing... I remember... they were in pain... his voice...?" He could hardly speak as his thoughts flitted from one memory to another. He closed his eyes and winced when he recalled the pain from Kanor's voice.

"A bloodstone saved us," said a voice from the doorway. Phoenix's eyes sprang open as Anolai entered the room.

"Anolai? What happened? What bloodstone?" Phoenix asked weakly.

"It protected Scarlyn from the mermaids and eased his pain when Kanor spoke. His spells managed to weaken Kanor until our pain subsided."

Scarlyn entered as he said this and added, "We all brought the ghoul down. I could not have done it alone."

Phoenix nodded, his mind clearing. "I was foolish to think I could," he said. "I am sorry."

"Just don't do it again," Mushbahc grinned as he entered. Aleya's cheeks flushed when she saw him.

Phoenix smiled. "I owe you my life, troll. I was no easy burden."

"No, but neither am I weak. I managed you well enough."

"Enough gabbing!" Galayvin exclaimed from the doorway, laughing. "Lord Almyn is waiting for us."

Phoenix immediately started to pull the covers back and Aleya quickly turned her back, blushing. Phoenix froze and the others chuckled.

"We'll meet ya down there," Galayvin laughed. Aleya was the first from the room, and the others followed, wide grins on their faces.

Several moments later, a large group assembled in the courtyards of the elfin embassy. Berinder and Lord Almyn stood upon a large stone slab facing the crowd. Kwea and Kundin stood by the roses, their faces serious and thoughtful. Phoenix, Galayvin, and Scarlyn stood together among the tiger lilies, conversing quietly. Mushbahc stood alone beneath a great tree, wordlessly listening to the murmur of the rest of the group and the whisper of the trees. Anolai and Elara stood silently beneath a gentle willow, the prince watching his father attentively. Krimple had left for his homeland many hours prior.

Aleya stood nearby, a bouquet of flowers in her slender hands, a look of serenity upon her charming face. Her soft hair and emerald gown blew in the gentle breeze. The setting sun cast rays of sparkling gold into her hair and the soft light draped a ruddy glow upon her cheeks. Occasionally, Mushbahc would glance at her, soaking up her ethereal beauty.

Almyn held up his hands and addressed the company. "You have all done well in retrieving the Amort Stone and in rescuing your comrades from the clutches of death. Now a second quest lies before you: to destroy the legendary sword, Tyrfing. To do this, you must journey into the heart of Nartok and to the lair of the dragon, Darrheil. This formidable foe will be a great danger to you, even in your combined strength. Though I wish I could spare him the journey, alas, Kundin must travel with you, for it is his touch that will destroy the sword." Almyn turned to Berinder and motioned him to speak.

"Darrheil is a very powerful dark dragon," Berinder told them. "Who, after he has slain them, raises the dead to serve him. Mushbahc knows the way to Darrheil's lair and will lead you to him." Mushbahc nodded respectfully to the wizard, and Berinder continued. "I shall journey

The Tale of Tyrfing

with you to aid however I can. The Amort Stone's power will render Darrheil's troops useless."

He paused. "However, it will destroy anyone who wields it." At this, the men looked anxiously at each other, then back to Berinder. "This will I do for you so that you may destroy the dragon and the sword."

"No!" Phoenix whispered hoarsely. His eyes were filled with a fearful, pained agony as he took a step forward then froze. Berinder looked at him, and their eyes spoke volumes. Lord Almyn stepped forward.

"I too, would join you, but I cannot. The nine of you must work together and muster the strength to defeat the dragon and his army. I send with you my blessings." The men's eyes flitted around the courtyard then Anolai turned and spoke.

"Father, there are eight of us..."

"Aleya will be traveling with you." Lord Almyn stated calmly.

"What?!" Galayvin and Phoenix cried.

"But, Father..." Anolai objected.

Almyn hushed them quickly with a raised hand. "Silence," he said calmly. "Aleya will be of greater assistance if she is one of your party. She can no longer aid you from afar."

"Forgive me, Lord Almyn," Mushbahc spoke respectfully. "But I do not understand."

Almyn smiled. "By whose magic do you think you were aided in the lagoon of the mermaids?"

"The boat?" Phoenix asked, surprised. All eyes turned to Aleya and she smiled and nodded.

After a short pause, Galayvin broke the silence. "Well, it sounds good to me," he said. He winked at Aleya and added, "Women have more power than most men give them credit for."   Aleya blushed and Galayvin grinned broadly, bowed to Almyn, and swaggered into the embassy. The others followed until Berinder and Almyn were left standing alone in the last rays of the golden sun. They were silent for a moment.

"May all be well with you," Almyn finally whispered. Berinder nodded as they firmly shook one another's hand. "And with you, dear friend," Berinder replied.

Berea was dark and quiet. Most of her inhabitants slept peacefully; others not so well. A few slept not at all and Phoenix Talrid was one of these few. The drow stole softly and silently across the elfin courtyards and into the city's silent, shadowed streets. Ever so quietly, he slipped down the dim alleys and bravely entered the darkened courtyards of the shadow elves. He found a vine beneath a window and began to climb.

By Sokarjo Stormwillow

Suddenly, as his head rose above a dark windowsill, a candle was lit and Phoenix looked up into the deep purple eyes of Nehru Tvildar. She laughed softly and her voice was as gentle music to his ears. His eyes grew wide and he grinned nervously, then suddenly lost his grip and fell. Crashing to the ground below, Phoenix groaned as new wounds were added to old. Nehru gasped and leaned out the window, a concerned look upon her face, her silky black locks falling softly past her shoulders. Quickly, she set the candle down upon a bureau and slipped out of the window. She grasped the vine and slid gracefully down the cold stone walls.

"Are you hurt?" she asked sweetly, kneeling by the intruder's side.

"Not badly," Phoenix admitted, humiliated.

"You should be more careful when spying on young girls," Nehru teased.

"I wanted to see your face once more," he said boldly, gazing at the figure before him that belonged to a young woman, not a girl.

"You're certainly honest," she blushed.

"I'm sorry. I do not mean to offend you," Phoenix apologized quickly.

"I do not take offense to honesty," the girl replied, smiling. She held out her hand to him and helped him rise. When he was standing, he continued to hold her hand, staring shamelessly into her eyes until she dropped them and blushed.

Phoenix let go of her hand. "I must beg your forgiveness once more, sweet maiden. Your eyes draw me as the sea is drawn to the moon."

Again Nehru blushed and smiled. "You speak flattering words," she murmured softly.

"I am certain a creature so lovely as you has heard many a flattering remark."

"Yes, though rarely do they come from a man bold enough to climb to my window." Nehru teased again, smiling up at him.

"In all honesty, I knew not which window was yours, but I..." At that moment, a voice came from within.

"Nehru? Nehru, where are you?"

"Father!" she gasped. She pushed Phoenix away. "Quickly! He mustn't find you!"

Phoenix reluctantly pulled back then snatched her hand again. "I'm leaving tomorrow on a quest, but I will return. May I see you again?" he whispered.

"Yes! Yes!" Nehru giggled. "Now go!"

Phoenix grinned and dashed into the shadows, just as a tall, regal figure appeared in the window. Long, ebony streams framed a stern, yet kindly face, set with onyx eyes.

"Nehru? Oh, Nehru, must you climb the walls in your dresses?" her father asked. "Come up here, it is late."

"Yes, Father," she said sweetly and grasped the vine.

"Nehru," Baral started to object, but his daughter had already begun her ascent.

Nearby, Phoenix watched as Baral lifted his daughter in through the window. Grinning, he limped back to his own quarters and slipped quietly into bed. That night, he dreamt of a beautiful maiden with silky, black tresses and deep purple eyes.

It was not yet dawn when the party passed through the enormous gates of Berea. The guards bowed low and the elf greeted them warmly.

"Good morrow, Lord Berinder," he said. "I wish you a pleasant journey." Berinder smiled solemnly at him.

Phoenix's joyful countenance drooped sadly for a moment as the irony of the elf's farewell struck him. All thoughts of lovely Nehru vanished, replaced by a fear for the wizard and a longing to protect him. His dispirited expression caught the attention of Scarlyn who left Galayvin's side and dropped back to speak to the drow.

"Why so sullen?" the wood elf asked.

Phoenix glanced at him, then up at Berinder who lead the party with Kwea and Kundin on either side of him.

"My heart cannot accept his fate," he finally sighed.

Scarlyn was thoughtfully silent for a moment. Phoenix turned and asked him a question. "What happened to the peasant who used the Stone against Kanor?"

Scarlyn hesitated, uncertain whether he should answer the query. But he did indeed speak the truth, saying, "He died. He was a good man, therefore, the Stone could not possess him – so it killed him. The spell on Kanor was only half worked, so the peasant's son snatched up the Stone. He died as well, but the work was done. The good die quickly, but the evil are possessed by the Stone's enticing power."

Phoenix mulled this over for a moment then spoke. "Then it is not Berinder who should use the Stone. A dragon as large and powerful as Darrheil will require just as long, perhaps longer, to work the magic on."

"You forget, it is not the dragon on whom he will use the Stone, but his minions," Anolai objected, entering the conversation. "The Amort Stone, if you recall, does not only curse the living with undeath, but the undead with annihilation."

"But there are many of them," Phoenix replied. "How will Berinder live long enough to destroy them all?"

There was a long, silent pause as Anolai and Scarlyn looked at each other anxiously. Then Anolai replied.

"I do not know."

Mushbahc led them safely, and without incident, through Bogok, the land of the trolls. They slipped quietly and undetected through the swamplands and marshes of that land, heartily wishing for clear water and solid earth. When first leaving the festering bogs of Bogok, the party were glad for the change in scenery. But it took little time for them to become just as fatigued and exhausted by the hot, dry desert wasteland that was Nartok.

For many long and tiresome days now, Phoenix had been troubled about the imminent battle with Darrheil. He had nightmares; horrible visions of the wizard's death, which woke him each night trembling in a cold sweat. The others began to notice the haggard weariness about the lad's face and demeanor. But no one spoke of why he was disturbed – they all knew.

One late night, after all the others had fallen asleep, Phoenix sat wide-eyed and alert by the fire, taking his turn to keep watch. Berinder slipped up and sat down beside his apprentice. They sat in silence for some time before either of them spoke.

"I would not have my passing trouble you, my lad," the wizard finally said softly.

"I wish I could the task away from you," Phoenix murmured, his voice full of pain and despair. "Is there no other way than the Amort Stone?"

"I fear not, my boy," Berinder replied sadly.

"Could we not search for one?"

"We do not have time," the wizard stated. "Kermain's forces already race us to the dragon's lair."

Phoenix paused in a sad, thoughtful silence. "Surely there is some sort of spell which will not destroy you!" he finally cried softly.

"Nay, have I not taught you enough?" Berinder asked earnestly. "Magic is not some sort of game to be trifled with, Phoenix. And magic involving death or undeath is the most dangerous of all! Even if we were to find a spell, it would destroy my soul, if not my body. In the end, it would be far worse than the destruction of my earthly form."

"Forgive me, Berinder. I know you speak the truth. I just wish it were not so."

"I understand your feelings, Phoenix, but this is the way of things, and for a reason. You must understand something, my boy: magic has the power to alter the structure of life and warp the very foundation of the cosmos."

"I understand," Phoenix nodded. "I understand."

Chapter Seventeen

Day after day passed with the red hot sun beating down mercilessly upon them. Dust filled their lungs and their bodies glistened with sweat. Their garments were filthy and worn. Every countenance drooped and each foot dragged wearily along. Only Mushbahc seemed to have the strength to journey on relentlessly. His alert, watchful eyes scanned the barren landscape for any sign of water or of trouble. His sense of smell was hampered by dust and ash, but his eyes and ears took up the slack, earnestly searching the horizon.

"Mushbahc!" Galayvin called. "Let the lady rest a moment!"

Mushbahc stopped and turned to face them. "We cannot stop. Please, m'lady," he added, turning to Aleya. "Let me carry you. I have ample strength yet."

Aleya shook her head. "No, I could not be such a burden to you. I can go on yet."

Mushbahc nodded. "If you should feel faint, please call to me and I will gladly bear you."

"After all," Phoenix laughed wearily. "He carried me all the way from Kanor's Mines. I am certain you would be a much lighter burden."

"That you would," Mushbahc heartily agreed, grinning.

They trudged on, persistent, pausing only for brief moments so the older gentlemen and the lady could catch their breath. Finally, Mushbahc stopped and turned to face them all.

"We will camp there tonight," he said, pointing to an outcropping of rocks on the face of a cliff. "We will burn no fire and there must always be a sentry this night. I will take the last watch. Tomorrow we will finish our journey to Darrheil's lair."

The group huddled up under the rock as night fell. There were no stars and no moon for the amount of ash and dust in the air, and the sky was quite dark. As the red hot sun ducked beneath the horizon, darkness brought with it a cold aridity. The drought of the land and the ash-riddled air were enough to keep Phoenix awake for quite some time. He had taken the first watch and sat huddled up, his back against the rocky wall, his mind wandering over tomorrow's adventure. By the time Galayvin stirred and sleepily told him to get some rest, the dark elf had arrived at a difficult decision.

The scorching sun had risen fully into the dusty sky when Mushbahc began to rouse the rest of the group. He paused at Aleya's side, taking a moment to soak in her peaceful beauty. Her long lashes rested calmly on pale cheeks, and a few stray strands of copper hair fell across her placid face. Her shoulders were round and smooth and Mushbahc wished strongly to just reach out and lightly touch that soft skin. Her body was stretched across the soft sand, and the folds of her garment and the light blanket caressed her curves rather than hiding them. Mushbahc inwardly chided himself for time spent, let his eyes linger a moment longer, then gently awoke her.

"M'lady," he said softly, touching her shoulder tenderly. "The hour has come."

Aleya stirred and her eyes fluttered open. Slowly she sat up, reaching out and resting her hand on Mushbahc's arm to keep him near her. "I had an odd dream, Mushbahc," she said, unaware of the stir she caused in his heart at the utterance of his name and the touch of her hand.

"I dreamt of a child, a blonde-haired child. He was being carried by a troll much more fearful than you, and at first, I feared for the little one. But when I looked behind the troll, I saw gruesome undead wolves giving chase and I realized the troll was trying to rescue the baby. Then I saw a shadow elf; he struck fear into my heart as none other has ever done. He was coming upon the child and I tried to rush forward to save him, but my fear had paralyzed me. Just as the elf's hand reached the baby, it was frozen, completely covered in ice. Then, before my eyes, the baby grew into a man, but I could not see his face. Just before I awoke, the ice on the drow's hand shattered and the image went black."

Mushbahc listened thoughtfully. When she finished, he paused then replied, "The child you saw was a barbarian babe, and the troll who saved him was my father. More than that, I have also had this same dream for the last few nights."

"As have I," Scarlyn said softly from nearby.

Aleya looked worried. "But what of the ice?" she asked. "And the hand? And what happened to the child?"

Kwea stepped up and answered her query. "I cast the spell that imprisoned the drow, trapping his spirit into an icy prison within the band he wore. I saw markings upon the band which I have never seen duplicated anywhere else."

The Tale of Tyrfing

By this time, the whole group had gathered round to hear. Berinder offered a suggestion. "Perhaps you could sketch the symbols in the earth with your staff, for all to see."

Kwea nodded. Gripping his staff with both hands, he proceeded to trace lines in the ashy dust at his feet. As he drew, everyone leaned in, watching attentively.

Before Kwea could finish the markings, Scarlyn looked up, startled, and glanced at Galayvin. The barbarian knew what the look meant and leapt forward, snatching away the Mazi's staff. The rest of the party watched in astonishment as he wordlessly filled in the remaining lines. Before anyone could speak, Galayvin quickly let go the staff to the ground, dropped to his knees beside the etchings in the earth, and began to pull off his shirt. The group gasped at what they saw. Tattooed upon his chest were the exact same symbols.

"I have borne these since I was a child. I have never known what they meant."

Berinder spoke after a slight pause. "I believe it is clear now what happened to the child rescued so long ago. Grimfar would never speak of the babe nor what had become of it, though the child's grandmother begged him in tears. He said he could never tell anyone... we all assumed the child must have died."

"My father never spoke of how Galayvin came to dwell among us," Scarlyn added. "His past was always a great secret, kept faithfully by our oldest druids."

Mushbahc watched silently, thoughtfully. Berinder nodded to Scarlyn. "Yes, things seem to be coming together now."

"But Berinder," Aleya wondered. "Why should I be having these dreams? Or any of us?"

"Because." Mushbahc replied before Berinder could. "Because he is back and he is looking for the boy... the man we all know. And I believe... He is killing again at this very moment."

All eyes turned on him, bewildered. "As I traveled from Kerik to Damor with Seaghan Jordahn, there was a night wherein I dreamt a fearful nightmare that caused me to awaken sharply. We were on the edge of a shadowed forest and I heard noises nearby. Seaghan followed me as I crept into the wood to see what was there. We saw a woman, a beautiful drow, who seemed possessed. Behind her, a phantom whose essence seemed to stream from a black band upon the girl's ankle, a band bearing those markings, and a long tail of black hair dangled from the phantom's arm."

Berinder nodded sadly. "That would be the band belonging to Galayvin's mother, Odenia, and the hair of his father, Brollen."

Anolai stood tall and spoke strongly; "Come, my friends. We have discussed this long enough. It is clear that we have much to learn and do about this evil necromancer and Galayvin's past. But today we battle a dragon and reclaim a cursed sword. We must carry on."

"Yes lad," Berinder agreed. "Let us carry on."

"Wait," Phoenix commanded. Everyone froze at the sound of his voice: fearful, yet authoritative; passionate, yet almost--- sinister. "First I have something to say. The Amort Stone will kill Berinder--- and it will kill him before he completes his task. I know this--- we all do. Berinder--- my dear friend and counselor--- you are too good a being to bear this accursed stone long enough to destroy the dragon's army. It is not my fear nor my inability to accept your death that makes me say this--- it is a truth we all know. So hear me and heed what I say, for it has taken much thought to reach this decision. My father was drow, my mother an elf of light; Berinder's guidance and influence upon me has brought out the nobility of my mother's race, my past has exposed the evil of my father. I am the child of forced rape, the bastard son of a moonless night. My father's depraved blood courses through my veins, mixed with the sunlight of my mother's stolen innocence. It is this combination that I know will keep me from being possessed by the Amort Stone, while preserving my life long enough to do the work. For our mission to succeed, the minions must be completely destroyed, leaving the dragon unprotected. For this reason, I will use the stone."

There was a long silence as Phoenix searched each face, and each of his friends looked deep into his fiery eyes. Finally, Berinder nodded slowly. "So be it. My lad, you have learned all I can teach you in this life--- I believe you are ready for the next journey--- the one beyond this plane."

"Thank you, Berinder. I will never forget you or your wisdom." Phoenix's voice was softer, but no less resolved and determined.

"Well, then. Let's go!" Galayvin grinned. His smile appeared to always light his face, often seemingly unaffected by bad news or sad events. And this time, his mood helped everyone pull themselves together and gather up their things for the last leg of their journey.

As everyone was preparing to embark, Phoenix slipped over to Aleya and began to murmur softly to her. Leaning close he whispered secrets in her ear.

Mushbahc glanced at them. Seeing Phoenix speaking to Aleya so earnestly piqued his curiosity and he strained to pick up pieces of what they were saying, but to no avail. Yet he thought it odd that Phoenix leaned so close, touching the princess upon her arm, whispering in her ear. Moreso, Aleya's eyes lit up in delighted gaiety, then seemed to instantly drop under the crushing reality of what was to happen to Phoenix. Then, as Phoenix

The Tale of Tyrfing

pulled slightly away, she leaned up and kissed him, softly upon his cheek. Mushbahc turned quickly away, lest the two notice his interest. He could not begin to describe the pain and anguish his heart felt as it shattered within his chest.

Little did he know, that Aleya was not the object of the passionate fire in Phoenix's eyes, nor that the kiss Aleya gave the lad meant nothing more than to show that she understood and cared and would deliver the message he had whispered in her ear. He could not know that he had no reason to despair; and she did not see his glance or realize what the troll had witnessed. She could not know what was passing through his mind, or what was happening within his heart. And so, oblivious of the true nature of things, the two pressed on towards a likely death; the troll thinking he had lost the light of his world, and the elfin princess wondering why he would no longer look into her eyes.

The last few miles to the dragon's lair were the harshest they had traveled since entering the lands of Nartok. The dryness tore at their eyes, ripped at their skin and settled in their hair. The wind whipped at the torn edges of their garments, and the sun beat down mercilessly upon their already burning bodies. Aleya asked Berinder if she should cast a spell to cover the sun with clouds, but Berinder quickly said no, explaining that the odd weather would alert the dragon's horde to their presence too early, and adding that she should conserve all the magical energy she had for the battle ahead. And so they pushed on, taking shelter as often as possible in the shade of the jagged rocks protruding from the cliffs above them.

Finally, an appalling scent wafted around them, emanating from a huge, dark hole in the side of the cliff wall. The smell of death was so thick and heavy in the air, Aleya had to swallow hard to keep from losing her meager breakfast. The group paused as the revolting smell sent their stomachs and imaginations to quite undesirable places. As soon as they regained strength and resolution, the band pressed onward, approaching the menacing cave.

Aleya and Berinder wove a shield of invisibility around them all. "We have to get to the center of the horde before we unleash the Stone," Berinder quietly instructed. "And at the center of the lair, is the dragon. If we use the Stone near him, it might weaken him, as well as destroying his army."

"Certainly worth a try," Phoenix nodded. "But the dragon will use his fire."

"Leave that to me," Kwea responded. "I can give you a shield of ice and magic."

Phoenix nodded and Galayvin added excitedly, as if a child, "What do the rest of us do?"

"Remain hidden," Berinder told him. "And wait for my signal. As soon as I motion to you, unleash everything you have upon that dragon. Kundin may remain behind the rocks, for if he were to die, all hope for this mission would be lost. As soon as the dragon dies, we must search quickly for the sword. Without its keeper, the cave will quickly begin to crumble."

Everyone nodded. "One more thing," the wizard added. "Take nothing except the sword, Tyrfing. All treasure is cursed to the living. Leave everything else behind."

Within Aleya's spell of invisibility, the group trudged silently and carefully along the rocky, bone-littered path, moving deeper within the cave. Presently, they heard a dry rattle echoing from around a nearby bend.

As they rounded the corner, a gruesome and unsettling sight met their eyes. Before them stretched a massive cavern, lit by the light of a thousand torches, all casting menacing shadows upon the glittering cave walls. Scattered throughout the immense cavern were forges, built and run by undead, their blazing fires adding to the already intense heat. At each forge, a group of corpses slaved away, building amour and weapons, jewelry and goblets. They used the finest molten gold and silver, along with other metals the living did not recognize. Some were skeletons, long dead and bereft of all flesh and muscle. And yet they kept their eyes. Unholy eyes they were; lacking all color and thought, blanched white and unnatural. Only their bodies were there and working-- it was clear their souls had long since parted this earthly plane. Other carcasses were still decomposing, their dead flesh melting away, hanging from their bloodied bones. The bare skeletons were horrid enough, but the undead who still carried some flesh were more grotesque than any of them had or could ever have imagined. The men glanced concernedly at Aleya, whose face had blanched white. Galayvin touched her shoulder and whispered.

"Are you alright?" The princess nodded, gulping hard.

Their hearts pounded in their ears as they carefully skirted the busy, rocky courtyard. Softly, they crept down another long passageway littered with bones and flesh and scraps of metal. The smell was almost unbearable, but slowly they were becoming accustomed to it. They forced themselves to concentrate on stealth and the battle ahead, doing their best to ignore the scent and sight of the gore around them.

Finally, they knew their destination was at hand; the heat increased to almost intolerable levels, and Aleya and Kwea had to work together to stave off the boiling waves.

Berinder whispered to them all. "The invisibility will not work on the dragon. We should stay out of sight until Phoenix touches the stone." All nodded.

Berinder stopped and put his hand on Phoenix's shoulder.

The Tale of Tyrfing

"Your life, though not long, has taught you many things; do not forget them. I swear to you, by moon and stars and brilliant sun, that if any of us should escape this hell, your name and deeds will be recorded and sung of for ages to come. More so, your memory will linger with all of us until we each pass from this earth, and ever after. May your next journey be one of strength and greatness."

As soon as Berinder gave his blessing, Aleya tossed her arms around the shadow elf. Clutching him tightly, she whispered words only he could hear and understand. "I'll always remember you... and so shall Nehru." The mention of her name brought a faint blush to Phoenix's face and a sparkle to his eyes, which did not go unnoticed by Mushbahc. Still, the troll, while admitting defeat to himself, approached the drow and warmly gripped his hand, gazing deep into his black eyes. Wordlessly, he stepped aside as Galayvin wrapped Phoenix in a barbarian-style bear hug, lifting him slightly off the ground.

Each member of the party gave their farewell, silently, but full of emotion and warmth. Phoenix smiled on them all and returned each embrace with his own.

Finally, Berinder slipped a leather pouch into his hand. Phoenix could already feel the evil ooze from the stone. "Time is short," he said and the party scrambled quickly behind rocks in the dragon's innermost chamber. They had spread out a bit, but not so far as to lose sight of Berinder or Phoenix.

Here, the dragon lay, eyes closed in slumber, smoke curling up from his nostrils. As deep silence fell over the somber group of warriors, Kwea worked quickly to fashion a shield of ice and protective magic. To this shield, Berinder added his own powers of protection, as did Aleya.

Finally, Scarlyn removed the bloodstone from around his own neck and slipped it over the drow's head. "It aided us before, I pray it will do so again," he murmured as the mithril chain settled on Phoenix's grey neck.

At long last, it was time for the battle to begin. Phoenix clutched the pouch in one hand, and the bloodstone necklace in the other. Gravely he nodded to Berinder and the wizard stepped forward and grasped the edges of the pouch. "Farewell, my son." He spoke softly then jerked the pouch from around the Stone, letting it fall into the drow's open palm.

Instantly, a raging, red blaze shot up around Phoenix's form. Screaming once in pain, Phoenix clenched his teeth and braced himself. The moment the unholy fire wrapped around him, the most hellish shrieks resounded through the rocky halls. The dragon awoke and roared, and the rest of the group covered their ears at the sound. But their eyes remained open, alertly watching the wizard for the signal to attack.

The shadow elf's eyes blazed red as he clutched the two stones in each hand. The dragon roared again, and this time his protest sounded more of pain and less of anger. As well as destroying the undead, the Amort Stone seemed indeed to be weakening the dragon, or at least giving him considerable pain. Berinder knew the time had come, and raised his staff and shot a single bolt of white light at the dragon's right eye.

Judging this to be the signal, the rest of the warriors leapt into action. Aleya began drawing shapes and runes in the dust at her feet, murmuring incantations of binding and pain upon Darrheil. Anolai leapt to his feet and drew his bow. Arrows dipped in liquids of light and magic sped from his longbow, pelting the dragon's face and neck. Kwea, spitting words in his own native tongue, shot bolts of ice at the dragon, hitting mostly his eyes, face, and joints. Scarlyn, Galayvin and Mushbahc leapt at the beast, scrambling up his towering limbs and mounting his glistening back. Galayvin raised his huge claymore and pelted the legs of the russet dragon with fierce blows. Mushbahc gripped his battleaxe with both hands and swung it at the back of the dragon's brawny neck, attempting to sever the spine.

All the while, the dragon writhed around, swinging his great tail, bellowing angrily, and blowing smoke and fire at the rock walls of the cavern. The Stone had weakened his eyesight and he could no longer determine who, what, and where the attacks were coming from. Scarlyn leapt with great agility up the dragon's neck, perching precariously upon his head and driving a dagger into the dragon's body to help him hold his position. He began hacking with his short sword at the beast's eyes and blood gushed from the dragon's many wounds. Finally, with a great roar, Mushbahc swung his blade deep into the brown dragon's flesh and severed his neck. With a great low groan and a terrible shudder, the giant beast fell hard to the ground, sending a quake through the rocky caverns.

The great and terrible Darrheil was dead.

But the day was not over. Immediately, the walls and ceiling began to crumble and collapse. Above the sound of the caving lair came a hideous, spine-tingling scream of pain and death. All eyes turned to Phoenix, still wreathed in flame and clutching the Amort Stone. Aleya took a step closer then stopped, the anguish in her eyes matching that of his cries. As the flame blazed up and Phoenix vanished from their sight, Aleya dropped to her knees and burst into tormented tears. Instantly, the unnatural blaze extinguished completely, leaving a pile of charred bones and ash.
Berinder turned quickly to the rest. "Find the sword!" he cried out.

Obeying immediately, the rest of the men scrambled about, searching for the mythical weapon. "Aleya, come quickly," Berinder commanded. The princess darted quickly to his side, wiping the tears from her eyes. "Open the bag," he ordered hurriedly. Aleya nodded and untied an empty satchel from the wizard's belt. Stepping quickly to where Phoenix had stood, the wizard

The Tale of Tyrfing

began mumbling mysterious words, pointing his staff at the pile. Holding the pouch open wide, Aleya watched in wonder as Berinder's magic lifted the bones into the air, swirling about and drawing towards her trembling hands. As he moved his hands, the bones and ash followed, stopping above the open satchel and dropping lightly inside. Quickly, she drew the strings and handed the bag to Berinder. Taking it, he lashed it firmly to his belt and turned back to the spot. Being careful not to touch the Amort Stone, Berinder lifted up the mithril chain bearing the bloodstone and gazed at it. Where Phoenix's fingers had clutched the stone, there were dark stains of purple that did not fade.

Just then, a shout came from below them. "I found it!" Galayvin cried, joyfully.

"Come along!" Berinder replied. "We have no time! Let's get out of here before we all perish!"

The men ran quickly to him and they fled the crumbling cavern. Weaving their way through piles of bone and rotting flesh, the group made their way as quickly as possible to the lair's entrance. A deep rumble from behind told them they had little time to escape. Scarlyn murmured quietly and formed a shield above them, similar to the one that had sheltered them in Kanor's Mines. But he was weak and weary from the battle and sadness, and his shield wavered.

Suddenly, they saw light ahead and rushed towards the flickering radiance. Just as the cave was collapsing, the group emerged from the dusty depths and fell, tumbling, down the embankment before the gap. Relief poured over them as soon as they realized they had all escaped with their lives.

But their delight was short-lived. As the dust settled they saw that they were not alone. Surrounding the lair, stretching for many miles around them, stood a silent, fearsome army of trolls, shadow elves and orcs. Their hearts dropped to their knees and they gazed around them in terror. A warg approached them, a disfigured drow atop its back.

"Greetings, adventurers." He seethed at them. "I am Slythe, general of the army of King Kermain of Piyr. Surrender the sword or die."

Chapter Eighteen

Shouts echoed down the long halls. Soldiers barking orders to one another, women sobbing as they were hurried into safer parts of the castle. The sun was sinking slowly toward the horizon, and torches were lit to shed light on the advancing troops. It was a small militia, to be sure, but much larger than the handful of men that occupied the city. Kilme gave orders to seal the doors as soon as the peasants were inside. He ushered the young king into the garden, and ordered soldiers posted in concealed locations. He was strapped in amour, a sword by his side, as was Seaghan, who wore Kilme's old sword at his hip. Seaghan darted to the memorial for his family and firmly planted his feet in the soft, newly turned soil, awaiting his uncle's arrival.

Sometime after dark, the castle was breeched. Seaghan shook as he heard the all-too familiar voice of his uncle shouting orders to his troops to smash down the door to the garden. Kilme glanced at him.

"Courage, lad, courage." Seaghan nodded.

Finally the door shattered and a small portion of Kermain's troops stormed in, surrounding Kilme, Seaghan, and what few soldiers were standing near them. Kermain strode in, an evil grin on his face.

"Good evening, Kilme," he spat, bitterly. The scar on his face stood out sharply in the flickering torch light. He glared at Kilme for a few seconds, then turned and gazed venomously at Seaghan. "And this must be my darling nephew," he grinned maliciously. "The one who escaped…"

Seaghan glared back, not looking away for a moment and not uttering a word.

"Well, boy. What do you think of your old uncle? Quite a sight, am I not?"

"You are a murderer," Seaghan said softly, indignantly. "You are no uncle of mine."

Kermain laughed, a wicked, jarring laugh. "Am I not?" Sarcastically he added, "ah, now boy, you're breaking my heart."

"I hardly think so," Seaghan replied coolly. "That would require you to have one."

Kermain grinned devilishly. "This lad is sharp," he said to Kilme. "It's a pity I must kill him." This last he said as he glared spitefully at Seaghan.

Kilme drew his sword and stepped between Kermain and the boy. "Over my dead body," he challenged. Kermain's soldier's stepped forward, but a wave of Kermain's hand held them back.

"My pleasure," he snarled, taking a step towards Kilme. At that instant, a horn blew, and Kermain's eyes widened. He stepped quickly to the wall behind him and looked down into the courtyard. Guresh's troops were swarming the grounds and already Kermain's forces were quickly losing control. Gren looked up into Kermain's livid face. "Up there!" he cried, pointing.

"Go ahead!" Kermain jeered. "See if you can get to me before I kill your precious nephew, coward!"

His arrogance cost him dearly.

As Kermain was mocking Gren, Kilme leapt forward with a speed remarkable for his age. A quick slash with his sword and Kermain lost his sword arm at the wrist. He cried out in pain and dropped to his knees, clutching what was left of his bloody arm. His soldiers lunged towards him, but were halted by Kilme's hidden militia.

"Go ahead, old man," Kermain growled. "Do it."

"I have scarred your face and taken your hand. But it is not I who will draw your lifeblood." Kilme stepped back and Seaghan stepped before his uncle, Kilme's old sword in hand.

"You're going to make a child do it, eh?" Kermain sneered. "Not enough spine, old man? Or do you just want to keep your hands clean?" Kilme struck him with his fist across the jaw.

Seaghan cut in. "He is not forcing me to do anything against my will," he said coldly. "I told him the task was mine."

"Did you now?" Kermain scoffed.

"You are well-positioned, uncle." Seaghan spat the word as if it were poison to his lips. "Here, on your knees before the eyes of my mother, you will die; your vile blood will soak the earth beneath the stone memory of the innocent lives you slaughtered."

"Life is a fragile state, whelp. One that is easily altered," Kermain snarled, blood forming at his lip.

The Tale of Tyrfing

"Which makes it all the more precious," Seaghan replied. "A noble man fights only other men. For the slaying of defenseless women and children, you will die dishonored and despised. The Gods will close the gates of Valhalla to you, and you will wander lost in cold mists, cursed for eternity."

"What would a child know of Valhalla?" Kermain scowled, spitting blood at Seaghan's feet.

But behind his bitter façade of hatred, Kermain trembled in fear. Seaghan looked past his eyes and knew.

"Vengeance is mine," he declared, and swung Kilme's sword with all his young might.

Gren burst breathless through the garden doorway, just as Kermain's severed head rolled through the grass.

They were chained, hand and foot, and led roughly through the barren wastelands of Nartok at the pitiless hands of Slythe's orcs. Berinder, Kwea, and Kundin struggled to keep up, their ages showing in their weakness after battle. But they were braced by the other men, who did all they could to help them endure.

Aleya was chained as well, but was compelled to ride a horse at Slythe's side. She stared straight ahead and spoke not a word to the elfin general.

After a long period of silence, Slythe spoke to her. "Such an expression does not become you, m'lady." His voice was dripping with suave charm and persuasiveness. Aleya did not answer.

"One so fair as you must surely..."

"You need not waste your treacherous words on me," Aleya interrupted.

Slythe smiled wryly. "I see," he replied.

Aleya glanced sideways at him, then down at Tyrfing dangling from his horse. She looked quickly away, but Slythe had seen. "Are you planning something, my dear? Some sort of foolish, heroic delusions of grandeur?" Aleya was silent. "Just remember, princess, each time you attempt to escape or to free your friends, one of them will die."

"If you are so eager to shed their blood, why keep us alive?" Aleya asked, coldly.

"King Kermain requested that, if possible, I should bring you all back alive. If not, you and the sword will do splendidly."

"Why me?"

"My lord is about to become king of Damor... he will need a queen." As he said this, the drow touched her cheek. She jerked away and glared icily at him.

"I would rather die," she seethed.

"Perhaps," Slythe replied, still smiling coolly. "I will leave that decision to the king."

That night, the group huddled together around a fire, still in chains and guarded by two very unpleasant orcs and a grim-looking troll. Aleya tried to heal their wounds as best she could, grateful the guards did not try to stop her. As she finished, however, the troll stepped towards her, and she drew back slightly in fear. But the troll stopped before her, bared his leg, and motioned toward an ugly cut. Aleya worked quickly to heal it, and the troll grunted and stepped back.

"Why did you do that?" Kundin asked.

Aleya shrugged. "I saw no need not to," she replied, casually. The answer did not seem to be enough for the men, so she added, "I am a healer. That is what I do."

A couple hours later, the three guards were asleep, along with the rest of the camp, the orcs snoring loudly. Aleya slept as well, but the rest of the prisoners were wide awake.

"We can't just sit here and wait for death," Galayvin said, softly, but firmly.

"Well we can't just get up and walk out of here," Anolai retorted. "And we can't leave Tyrfing."

"Yes," Scarlyn agreed. "We must destroy the sword."

"But what if it makes a sound?" Anolai asked. "What if it wakes the camp up? Then we'll never escape, and likely be killed for destroying, or at least attempting to destroy the sword. How do we even know that Kundin merely touching it will be enough to destroy it?"

"Because Berinder says so," Galayvin stated. "And that's good enough for me."

Berinder smiled. "Thank you for the confidence, my friend," he replied. "But Anolai asks a good question. I take no offense. My companions have known since Tyrfing first vanished that it would resurface someday. As soon as it was lost, the head of my order visited Dvalin and Durrin, the forgers of the sword. They were asked how to destroy the weapon, should it be found. They said all they had to do was touch it, and the entire sword, blade and hilt, would shatter into dust. They also said that if they were no longer living, that one of their descendants would have the same effect. Kundin is the last living of their lineage."

Galayvin nodded. Anolai spoke up, "This is all well and good, but how should we proceed? We must destroy that sword, before it ends up in the hands of a bloodthirsty murderer like Kermain." So earnest were they in debating their next move, none of the men, even the keen-eared elves, heard the snoring that rumbled from the guarding troll's belly, silence.

"We must get Aleya out of here. We can't let her be killed, or mercilessly handed over as a bride to that brute. And someone has to stop Nakasuin from destroying Piyr. If the sword does shatter into dust, it is likely it will waken our slumbering captors."

"Yes," Kundin nodded. "Highly likely. But I am old and have lived my life long and well. Yet I leave behind no legacy, save for this. If I am to die, let it be in accomplishing the greater good, and destroying the accursed sword, Tyrfing."

The rest nodded, admiring the dwarven lord's courage. A voice above them startled them all and sent shivers down their spines.

"No need die," came the short, simple words from the troll standing menacingly above them. Their hearts sunk into their stomachs.

But they were not ready for the troll's next words.

"Hepfar help," he grumbled quietly.

The Tale of Tyrfing

Chapter Nineteen

The night stars were winking in the silent sky above the dusty terrain. There were no sounds of night animals; only the dry wind that brushed over the sandy soil. For miles, there was nothing but short, scraggly brush and barren rocks. There was no where to hide, no where to run.

But that did not bother them. Aleya's spell of invisibility would hide them from their hunters. And with the aid of Hepfar, who happened to be a trollish shaman, they would be able to move quickly over the ground; much more quickly than their pursuers. Hepfar's spell for flight would see to that. It was the stealing and destruction of the sword that would be the most difficult task.

Mushbahc would steal the sword and they would get as far away as possible before destroying it, hoping to buy some time. Should Slythe awake, first of all, he would see a troll and not consider the possibility that it was one of the prisoners. Second of all, if he should happen to recognize Mushbahc, the troll could throw the sword to Kundin who would promptly destroy it. It was a very risky venture, but one they had to undertake; the sword had to be destroyed.

Mushbahc crept as silently as he could up to the shadow elf's tent. All was dark within. Parting the tent flaps just enough, he peered in and immediately saw Tyrfing laying beside Slythe's mat. He took a deep breath and gently let it out; softly, he stole into the dark tent.

Kundin stood ready at the tent's doorway, crouched low and huddled in the shadows. Mushbahc inched his way towards the mat Slythe was sleeping on. He listened carefully to be sure the drow's breathing was even and deep. In his hand, the troll clutched a sword, of similar size to Tyrfing, which Hepfar had given him. If Slythe awoke during the night, if he was drowsy and did not look hard, he would not immediately be alerted to Tyrfing's absence. For all his simple speech, Hepfar had truly thought of everything.

Mushbahc was standing next to Slythe's mat now, barely breathing. Slowly, carefully, he lifted Tyrfing and replaced it with the broadsword in his hands. Just as slowly as he had entered, Mushbahc edged cautiously from the tent. Slythe stirred once, grunting and growling to some unseen threat. But he slept on, unaware of what was taking place mere inches from his deformed face.

The moment Mushbahc exited the tent, he motioned to the elderly dwarf to follow him. Kundin leapt to his feet and scurried after him quietly. They returned to the rest of the group, "guarded" by Hepfar, and waited there for a moment to see if anyone stirred. None did.

Quietly and softly, Aleya worked her magic. In moments, the entire party was invisible. Then, Hepfar began to weave his spell, the group huddled around him. His voice low and gruff, Hepfar mumbled a few words in a primitive language. The dust beneath their feet stirred a bit, then they lifted into the air. Shortly, they were soaring across the ground, horizontal above the earth, seemingly on invisible wings.

A few miles away, behind a large rock, they paused, standing on air above the earth. Mushbahc held up the sword and spoke softly to the darkness, for they were invisible to each other as well.

"Lord Kundin?"

"Aye, I'm here lad," Kundin replied, stepping towards him.

"Lay Tyrfing upon that rock there," Berinder said. Mushbahc obeyed and it immediately became visible to all.

The dwarf reached out and took the legendary sword up in his hands. A bright light shone around the hilt and scaffold, and the fugitives were glad they were out of sight of the enemy camp. Then, in an instant, the light was gone and they all heard the soft sound of a small puff of air as the sword vanished.

There was a silent pause. Finally, Galayvin spoke.

"That's it?" he asked, sounding slightly disappointed.

Immediately, the whole group laughed heartily. Except Hepfar, who reminded them of their position.

"You stop, laugh," he complained, grimly. "Time fly."

"Then so must we," Kwea replied, smiling. "Let us hurry on. Berea waits and morning does not."

The wind blew their hair back, their speed was that more swift than a horse, but they did not tire. In fact, it was the most wonderful feeling Aleya thought she had ever felt. She had dreamt of flying like this many a night, and now it was reality. She reached out her arms, feeling the wind against her chest. She brushed someone and the touch of his scaly skin and leather amour told her who. The feeling of ecstasy made her brave and she slid her hand down his arm and grasped his claw-like hand.

The Tale of Tyrfing

"Close your eyes," Mushbahc whispered in her ear. "Trust me."

Aleya closed her eyes and smiled. She could feel herself speeding along the ground, the wind gliding over her skin, the sounds of the night air in her ears. She clung tightly to Mushbahc's big hand, delighting in the rough touch of his fingers against her smooth, slender ones. She put all her trust in him as they wove in and out through rocks and over bushes. The feelings that welled up within her breast were like nothing she had ever experienced before.

"Now open them!" Mushbahc whispered urgently.

Aleya's eyes flew open just as they soared up over a deep gorge and into the first rays of sunlight. Rosy pinks and golden beams dancing across a pale, cloudless sky greeted her exultant eyes, behind the black silhouettes of jagged rocks and crags. They twisted round and put the sun to their sides as they headed northwest towards Berea. The spell of invisibility was beginning to wear off and Aleya could see they were a short way behind and to the right of their comrades. It was a glorious morning already, and Aleya had never been happier than she was right now: gripping Mushbahc's hand, soaring low above the earth, and feeling the rush of a freed bird.

And she was certainly a lovely bird in Mushbahc's eyes. He gazed at her as she soaked up the beauty of the golden skies. His heart soared with his body as he felt the cool touch of her small hand in his. As she became clearly visible to him, he felt like a weary warrior who, after being in distant lands engaged in battle, sees his homeland once again. The sun in all its golden splendor held no match to her, this lovely elfin maiden with eyes of green and head of auburn locks. Deep within him, the troll's heart stirred in such a way as he had not felt his entire life, a passion even stronger than the love he had felt for Colly as he cradled the child in his arms. That had been the love of a guardian for a child... this was the ardor of a warrior for an angel, a damsel that made the Gods themselves long to be in her presence.

Mushbahc's enthrallment was cut short, for Hepfar had stopped and was waiting for them to catch up. The group of renegades crowded around him.

"Dis where part," he stated abruptly, as the last of them drew close.

Each of the men grasped Hepfar's hand tightly and warmly. Aleya leaned up and planted a kiss on his cheek, which brought a curious look to the shaman's eyes.

Mushbahc was the last to step forward. "How can we thank you?" he asked. "We owe you our lives."

Hepfar gripped Mushbahc's hand and replied, "Slythe say we 'tack elves, men. He not tell we 'tack troll. Troll not raise hand 'gainst troll. Dis how it be for long time, and Hepfar not change. Hepfar help troll 'scape; and help elf 'scape for healing cut. Dat been hurtin' Hepfar long time."

Aleya smiled sweetly at him. He nodded to her, then added. "You fly for long time now. Hepfar tink you make it one day 'way Berea. But watch for ogre."

"Thank you, Hepfar," Berinder nodded. "We will never forget your deeds."

"Den Hepfar done good job an elders be glad."

The others waved merrily as Hepfar trod heavily away from them toward Bogok.

"Let us hurry," Anolai said. "We should get as close to Berea as we can before the spell wears off." They all agreed and pressed forward.

Anolai pretended not to notice his sister's hand in the troll's, but he did.

Chapter Twenty

They were all gathered round the great table in Lord Almyn's hall once more. They were safe, unharmed, and now cleaned and well-fed; but their faces wore looks of deep sorrow and thoughtfulness. All was silent as they brooded.

Finally, softly, Lord Almyn addressed the sulking party.

"Your sorrow for your friend will ease; with time, the pain will subside." All turned to him, listening silently as he spoke. "Never forget his deeds, nor for what purpose he died. Tyrfing is destroyed. That threat is at an end. Kermain is slain and even now, his armies scatter. The trolls have shown strength in time of ill-will, a loyalty to their fellows which most would not have suspected. Each of you has gained strength; strength within yourselves, and a strength that comes from the bonds of friendship. Much good has come of this great adventure you have all shared." A feeling of peace filled each heart as the truth of Lord Almyn's words brought comfort to their pain. Lord Almyn continued. "But there is yet one more task to complete – Nakasuin must be destroyed."

There was a silent pause. Then Kundin spoke. "There is one more good that has come from this trial." All eyes turned to the dwarven lord in curiosity. "For many ages my clan – and I – have regarded the tale of Tyrfing, as well as others, to be myths; stories full of wisdom, yet lacking in factual truth. The elder magic of our ancestors have been lost." Berinder nodded knowingly. "But to find and destroy Tyrfing--- this has given me a belief and a confidence in that magic. I know how to use it, though I had little conviction in its power before. Were I to return to the mountains of Gamlin, I am convinced I could forge a weapon with the ability to destroy Nakasuin."

Save for Berinder and Almyn, the party sat up sharply, instantly alert, their eyes wide and questioning.

"Are you quite certain?" Kwea asked.

"I am," Kundin acknowledged resolutely. Berinder smiled wisely.

"Well then, let's get going!" Galayvin exclaimed, eagerly leaping to his feet.

"I hate to detain you, Galayvin," Anolai kindly objected. "But what of the older men? It is already late in the day; we should start our journey at dawn."

"But time is of the essence," Scarlyn argued. "What of Morrana? And the numerous lives Nakasuin's black magic could be claiming right now?"

Berinder grinned broadly. "Gather your things," he told the others. "We will meet outside the city gates in twenty minutes." With looks of bewildered curiosity, the group quickly obeyed, leaving Lord Almyn alone, smiling.

Aleya pulled Mushbahc into a small secluded room.

"I am not going with you this time," she told him softly. "I have an important message to deliver and must stay behind."

Mushbahc nodded solemnly. Aleya hesitated, then continued. "Will you be returning?" she asked, hopefully.

"You think I'll let a ghost stop me?" the troll grinned.

Aleya blushed and her gaze fell to the floor. "I just wanted to hear it from you," she replied quietly, smiling.

With his emerald hand and black claws, the troll lifted her chin up until their eyes met. His voice soft and low, he sent her heart reeling. "My dear princess... we will meet again."

A delighted smile lit up the elfin maiden's face and her green eyes sparkled with joy. Mushbahc could resist no longer and suddenly pulled her close to him in a fierce embrace, their lips locking passionately.

Anolai approached his father. Almyn stood silently on a veranda, gazing out over the gardens of the embassy. He waited wordlessly for his son to approach, hardly acknowledging his presence. Anolai stepped up beside him and stared down into the gardens, trying to form the words to express what he was thinking.

After a silent pause, Almyn spoke. "I leave for Élas upon the morrow, Anolai. Your sister will be going with me, as, I suspect, will Nehru. I am leaving this quest in your hands, my son."

Anolai nodded solemnly and hesitated a moment longer. When he finally addressed his father, he spoke softly, with a hint of curiosity in his voice.

"Father? Why could you not come with us to Nartok? We could have used your help."

"Of that I have no doubt, Anolai."

"So why remain behind, if you knew you were needed?"

"Anolai," Almyn turned to look into his son's questioning face. "It may

The Tale of Tyrfing

be difficult for you to understand, or accept. Often it is a good thing for youth, such as yourself and your new friends, to experience difficulties and trials. Strength does not come from an easy life."

"Even to the point of risking our lives, Father?" Anolai wondered, a little surprised.

"Yes, Anolai. Even to that point. Be assured, your life and that of your sister means much to me. But it was a test you and she were meant to endure, and both of you have emerged the stronger and wiser for it. I could not have aided you in a manner that would encourage such a thing."

Anolai looked down again thoughtfully. Finally he replied. "I do not fully understand you, Father. But I suppose I shall in time."

"Yes, Anolai. Perhaps in time..." And father and son stood side by side, gazing out onto the world, in silent understanding.

Aleya was gone; she had fled to Nehru's home hastily, lest her brother notice the deep crimson blush staining her cheeks, or the dancing light of romance in her eyes. The others had gathered round Berinder in an empty field outside the city, their eyes filled with questions, their lips uttering nothing.

When all had settled round him, the old wizard smiled. "What is your plan, Lord Berinder?" Scarlyn asked curiously.

Silently, with a teasing smile and twinkling eyes, Berinder stepped through the group, who fell behind him, still baffled. Then before them appeared a grand sight; a large gathering of great beasts landed before them, the leader taking a few steps forward to stand beside the wizard. They were gryphons; great bird-like creatures with the bodies of lions, great white wings, and the heads of enormous eagles. They were terrifying and powerful, yet regal and quiet, an air of elegance and wisdom in their demeanor and carriage. Berinder placed a hand on the neck of the great gryphon.

"This is Brawn-Illiahn, the king of gryphons--- and my close friend for many ages. He and his people have gallantly agreed to bear us to Gamlin, to Mount Roguk."

The powerful gryphons never tired, nor did they need to stop for food or drink, their strong bodies able to go days and weeks without nutrient or water. Their riders carried bread and wine with them, sustaining themselves as they traveled. Within two days, the party had reached the majestic mountains of Gamlin. They soared high above the perilous peaks of the dwarven land, finally landing before the heavily guarded, great stone doors of Mount Roguk, the home of the Kaladure Clan.

"Why couldn't we have taken this way to Nartok?" Galayvin asked, dismounting

"The gryphons are not beasts of labor," Berinder replied. "They are a race unto themselves, not to bend to the beck and call of any, not even myself. They have shown us great kindness in this service, and deserve your gratitude, my friend."

Galayvin nodded and bowed low to the beast who had carried him. The others bowed in thanks as well when they had dismounted, and the gryphons bowed their heads then flew away into the white, empty skies of Gamlin.

Thlungmal welcomed Kundin with open arms.

"My Lord!" he exclaimed. "'Tis good to have ye back." All the dwarves clustered round Kundin, eager to hear his tales of adventure.

"My friends!" Kundin called out. "The battle has not yet been won! We have work to do! Hulak, Yarlod, get the forges hot. Thlungmal, I am in great need of mithril, my friend, enough for a quiver full of arrows."

Thlungmal did not question, but nodded and hurried off, four more dwarves behind him. Kundin sent other dwarves out for more special items, then ordered a feast to be prepared for his guests.

At the great feasting table, the others looked around, seeing no sign of the dwarven lord. Anolai asked of his whereabouts from an old dwarf who poured his mead.

"My Lord be down at the forges," the elderly dwarf replied. "He is not to be disturbed."

Anolai nodded. "Very well, did Lord Kundin leave any instructions for us?"

"Only that ye should enjoy yerselves," Thlungmal told him. "An that ye shouldn'ta wait up fer him, as it may take all the night."

The rest nodded and finished their meal, laughing and talking amongst themselves.

Chapter Twenty-One

The next morning they were awakened early, before the sun had yet peered over the horizon. A damp cold still lingered in the quiet caverns of the mountain, and outside the mountain, the earth lay silent in the dew of morning. Kundin awoke them all himself. They had not passed the horn the night before, and were quite sober and well-rested, regardless of the early hour. Awake and alert, yet reverently hushed, the group gathered round the lord of the mountain.

"The phantom has been found," Kundin told them solemnly. "He and his captive are on the northern borders of Gamlin, nearing Srak. I believe we can catch him before his curse unleashes on too many barbarians."

"Do you have a plan?" Anolai asked, tentatively.

"I do," Kundin replied, nodding. The dwarves have friends in Gamlin besides their fellows. The mighty Yerrynahd will bear us to Nakasuin."

"Yerrynahd?" Anolai asked.

"The great harts of the mountains." Scarlyn answered. "They are large white stags who rove the mountainside. Their skill on the rocky peaks should help us move with great speed. And what, Lord Kundin, is your plan for destroying the phantom?"

Kundin motioned to a nearby dwarf, who brought forward a quiver full of shimmering arrows. Kundin took the quiver and nodded to the dwarf, who bowed in return. He turned and handed it to Scarlyn. "You are given the heavy task to fire as many of these as it takes into the heart of the phantom," he instructed. "I do not know if it will take one or the whole quiver full, but these are imbued with the power to destroy the undead, sending the phantom into obliteration. This is your charge."

Scarlyn nodded gravely, taking the quiver and strapping it to his back.

"We cannot just walk up to him and fire an arrow," Anolai objected. "He will sense us coming, and perhaps even sense the power of the arrows."

Kundin nodded in agreement. "Aye, that he might. I am hoping Galayvin and Mushbahc will distract him."

"What would you have us do?" Mushbahc asked.

"Very little," Kundin replied, shrugging. "The scent of your blood will drive him crazy enough, though you may have to remind him whom you are."

Galayvin and Mushbahc nodded in understanding.

"Very well," Anolai said. "Let us be off at once. We have a phantom to destroy and a maiden to save."

Each of them heartily agreed, and they were soon on their way, pounding hooves and wings to carry them swiftly toward Srak and Nakasuin.

Their ride seemed short, though they had covered many miles. They soon came upon small camps of barbarian scouts and trappers. All were dead, their flesh gone; all skeletons with gaping eyes and mouths. At each camp, Berinder spoke spells to give their spirits rest and keep the bones from rising in undeath; and at each camp, Galayvin bristled and seethed with anger and hatred for the demon they were hunting.

In time, they happened upon a small camp, as the cries of dying men were just fading from the air. Berinder immediately began his spells, as Anolai spoke the obvious.

"We are clearly catching up," he said. "Nakasuin has only just left this place."

Scarlyn was off the giant hart and kneeling near a narrow, half-hidden path into the trees. "Yes," he said. "And he went this way. These tracks are fresh... a woman's."

"I know where that path goes," Mushbahc told him, dismounting. "It ends at a glade, not three miles from here. The clearing is a druid's haven of sorts, surrounded by stones and runes."

"Perhaps the demon intends to increase his power," Anolai wondered. "But that seems an odd place to do so. I would think a burial mound would better serve him."

"Perhaps he can only feel the power, and cannot yet see what type of power the place holds," Kwea suggested.

"Whatever his reason," Mushbahc declared. "We need to get going and catch him while he is still weak from using his power. Galayvin, you and I will lead. He's got to sense us first. Scarlyn, Anolai, follow us, but not too closely, and stick to the trees and off the path."

The group left the Yerrynahd to paw the ground behind the camp and followed Scarlyn.

The path wove among the trees, newly traveled, yet covered in fallen leaves, brush, and vines. A cool breeze filtered through the trees around

The Tale of Tyrfing

them and churned the leaves at their feet. All was still and silent; not a bird sang, nor cricket chirped, nor creature stirred; only the wind dared move.

Suddenly, Berinder stopped and grabbed Mushbahc's shoulder.

"Something is coming!" he said in a whisper. "And fast!"

"He knows we're here!" Mushbahc returned, also in a whisper. "Scarlyn, get ready! Galayvin, hands to your sword, boy. Not sure what we're getting into, but she's coming and she's running."

Kwea and Berinder stood firm behind the troll and the barbarian, and Anolai leapt quickly into the trees opposite from Scarlyn and drew his bow.

"Don't fire until I say!" Mushbahc whispered to them.

Suddenly, a girl rounded the corner and stopped, mere feet from the waiting warriors. Her eyes were glazed over, perfectly white, and she seemed not to see anything.

"Morrana," Galayvin gasped and stepped forward. Mushbahc raised his hand to stay him.

Behind her floated the sinister ghoul; Nakasuin in all his evil essence. His eyes glowed red as he stared at the two warriors before him.

"Your scent is familiar," he finally said, his voice an eerie hiss. "I know you, but I know not how. Tell me, and I will ease the pain of your death--- perhaps."

Galayvin glared at him in hatred and anger, his voice was deep and threatening when he responded. "The hair that hangs from your arm, demon, once belonged to my father, Brollen. And the anklet that binds you was once my mother's."

"Ah," replied the demon maliciously. "Then you are the one who escaped; the child whom I did not know was there until too late."

"You heard the outraged cry of a troll," Mushbahc growled, uncertain of how he knew this. "The troll rescued the child and escaped into the woods of Gamlin, taking it to the wood elves who dwelt there. That troll was my father, Grimfar."

Nakasuin scrutinized him well, looking him up and down with his glowing eyes. "Ah," he returned. "You are a most unusual troll. You do not speak like a troll, nor do you act like one. I smell barbarian blood in you."

"My mother was Sitka, of the barbarian tribe of the far north. Her blood runs in my veins as well."

"I see," the ghoul answered, casually. "Then the souls of both your mothers now feed my fire. When your father died at the hands of the Minotaur of Uruz, she fled in fear... right into my waiting arms. Her bones have long graced the back of my throne."

Mushbahc's raged flamed up within him, his eyes flashed with fury and his hands trembled slightly. Yet he made no move.

"You have astounding control over your anger," Nakasuin remarked. "A trademark of the trollish race, to be sure. Very well. It is time your bones joined your mother's."

A fiendish green light swirled about the skeletal hands, and the red eyes shone brighter.

The fires of hell were unable to burn through the flesh of the troll however, thanks to the shell of ice and magic the wizard and the magician had encased his skin in so quickly. Mushbahc did not move or flinch, but stared right into the very eyes of death.

"I see you have come prepared," Nakasuin said, his voice quivering with controlled rage. "Very well, how do you propose to destroy me? More ice perhaps, Kwea Ankuhr?"

The magician stepped up. "You do remember me," he smiled sarcastically. "I am flattered."

A dull grey smoke hissed up from the phantom's body, as his eyes flashed hotly. "Of course I remember you," Nakasuin growled spitefully. "How could I forget the one who bound me in this hell?"

"It was an honor," Kwea replied.

"Enough!" Nakasuin screamed, the binding of his rage weakening. "You have not come thus far to insult me, have you? Get on with it."

"Very well," Kwea replied, stepping forward. Immediately ice completely covered the band gripping the girl's ankle.

"Master," she droned, fear tipping her voice.

"Fear not, sweet maiden. The ice can only chill. It hardy weakens me. Come now, Kwea Ankuhr. Surely you have more than that."

Suddenly an arrow whizzed through the air, slipping through the mists of Nakasuin harmlessly.

"What's this?" the demon screeched. "You try to harm me with arrows? Fool! No human weapon can harm me!" But the arrow had achieved Anolai's goal. The phantom moved Morrana between himself and the light elf. "Now shoot!" the raging phantom demanded. "Shoot and kill that which this barbarian loves!"

But the next arrow did not come from Anolai.

Nakasuin screeched in terror and pain. He looked down at the bright mithril arrow lodged in his chest.

"WHAT?!?!" he shrieked, his unholy voice filling the wood. "THIS CANNOT BE!" Immediately, the mist around him began to evaporate, leaving him a physical being again, yet still pierced with the magic arrow. The white left Morrana's eyes and she sank slowly to the ground, unconscious. Galayvin leapt to her side and caught her, dropping

The Tale of Tyrfing

to his knees and letting his sword fall to the ground beside him. Nakasuin dropped to the ground, landing on his back, and his hand touched the shaft of the arrow. "The dwarves have lost their power and magic!" he continued wailing. "This is impossible!"

Mushbahc approached him. "Magic is never truly lost," he sneered in contempt. "Merely forgotten... able to be remembered."

"NO!" the phantom wailed, as blood began forming at the mark. "THIS CANNOT BE!"

Another mithril arrow flew through the air with incredible aim, striking right next to the first. The drow gurgled, blood trickling from his mouth. He tried to say something else, then his eyes blanched white.

The life left him.

Mushbahc turned and looked at Berinder. The wizard nodded and Mushbahc stepped forward. Raising his ax high, he swung and severed the drow's head at the neck. Lifting the head up by the hair, the troll dropped it into an empty sack he pulled from his belt. Then he turned and joined the rest of the group as they crowded around Morrana lying limply in Galayvin's arms.

Slowly, the beautiful shadow elf maiden lifted her ebony eyes. She looked blankly around, then reached up and touched Galayvin's face.

"I know your face," she whispered softly, weakly smiling. Galayvin looked up at Mushbahc, a confused look on his face.

Mushbahc looked sadly down at her and shook his head. "She is blind, Galayvin," he told him softly. Galayvin looked painfully down at her, then clutched her tightly to his chest, tears staining his cheeks.

The Tale of Tyrfing

Year One of the Dragon Age, Piyr, Midgard

Many miles away, in the harsh land of Nartok, the barren lands were giving way to lichens, then to grasses and bushes and trees. The fruitfulness of the land returned. Water streamed from long-dry rocks, old river beds began to fill again. The death of Darrheil had given life to the land once more, as it had been in ancient days. Things were beginning to change.

And deep within the earth, buried under a collapsed dragon lair, another change was resting. A change that had to grow, to develop, before it could greet the world, or even the light of day. A change that had witnessed the demise of Darrheil through mist-covered eyes. A change that would challenge the world of Piyr, and seek to revenge the death of Darrheil.

A change that lay nestled quietly within the protective shell of a dragon's egg.

CPSIA information can be obtained at www.ICGtesting.com
Printed in the USA
LVOW13s1856060813

346587LV00003B/657/P